To enjoy,

Ariel's Tear
A Tale of Rehavan

By

Justin Rose

Sing to me, nymphs of the river!
Sing to me, sprites of the wood!
Sing me the song of the Father,
Who purged your lands in his blood.

Stanza I of "The Lay of Reheuel"

Acknowledgments

As my first published novel, *Ariel's Tear* marks an exciting moment in my life, the fulfillment of a goal held for many years. Here in the book's first pages, I wish to thank a few of the many people who have helped me reach this goal.

Thank you

to Anna Goodling for always being there to encourage me, for reading and critiquing every draft of every story and every novel I ever pushed at you, and for constantly believing in my abilities;

to Abraham Feldick for the beautiful cover art that adorns this book;

to Will LaValley for the author photograph on the rear cover;

to all my classmates in the 2015 Professional Writing class at Pensacola Christian College, particularly Serena Rose who helped proofread this work;

and to all those dear friends in my life who have helped foster and cultivate my love of writing during the years I've spent learning the craft, particularly Rebekah Cullum and Coartney Freeland.

Table of Contents

On Creation

Deep in the murk of irreality, Faeja stirred restlessly. Before the light was known, neither was the darkness. Only Faeja. Intellect breathing in the nether preceding time.

Loneliness, a feeling then unnamed, pricked His soul, and He dreamed. Unwinding a thread of His essence, He cast it forth into the void and named it *time*. Eternally it grew and crept away from Him, drawing in the wake of its seconds subtle traces of Himself. Every second lessened His being which had once seemed infinite, unwinding His thread of self.

But still he created. For He loved the newness, the brevity of current, past, and future. A frail and filtered reality beneath His former plane. Existence devoid of the eternal—a novel and ingenious beauty.

Despite this new wonder though, loneliness persisted, a hunger unsatisfied with simple time. So Faeja drew them forth. Out of His soul He formed the Passions and the Traits to dwell in His new creation. They were beings of Faeja's own ether, each Passion and each Trait representing an element of His fuller being. Curiosity came first, followed by Love and Malice. And then came the rest, hundreds and thousands of names now forgotten: Lust and Generosity, Cruelty and Kindness, Guile and Honesty— they slid like glass beads upon the thread of time and made their way along its course. They met with one another and mingled, each interaction altering those involved, each perception of another passion diluting the purity of he who perceived. By these dilutions, the Passions and the Traits developed into conscious beings, ruled by their first natures but broadened to encompass all emotion.

Faeja smiled, but He desired more. He desired a stage, a reality to frame the intellects that dwelt in time. So, He created matter in the form of spiraling spheres and molded bodies to house the souls of His first children.

Ever forward, Curiosity was the first to alight upon a world in the new universe, the first to find that he could touch. And finding touch, he wanted more. He wanted to mold and to alter just as Faeja Himself had done. So, Curiosity approached the throne of Faeja and begged Him for the gift of creation.

Faeja smiled on Curiosity's request and unbound from His own essence a small portion of His creative force, His cyntras, to give to His favored son. Curiosity, still awed with the sensation of touch, used this borrowed cyntras to create new senses that would complement touch: sight, hearing, taste, and smell. All of his fellow Passions and Traits reveled in these sensations for a time. But the matter of first creation was too uniform to long hold their fascination. They approached the throne of Faeja as a body and begged Him for more creative power.

Pleased with Curiosity's creations, Faeja removed all the cyntras of His being, all His creative force, and bound it into the strings of a mighty Lyre. This Lyre He handed down to His children, content to watch them play the tunes of creation.

For a time, the universe continued in harmony. Curiosity used the Lyre to ply the music of reality. With the vibrations of the strings, new melodies sprang forth from matter. Atoms and molecules multiplied and formed into elements. Stars and planets discovered their orbits, and the universe began its eternal expansion outward from the Lyre. Creation was a symphony, written for the delight of its own musicians.

Imagination alone grew discontent with Curiosity's music. Seeing the eternal repetition of old scales and familiar chords, Imagination begged to take the Lyre that he might discover new melodies. With the Lyre, he crafted life. Plants came first, practice for the coming wonders. Then came the naiads and the dryads, spirits for the rivers and the trees. Fire Sprites rose from the notes of the lyre and fell to fester in the crust of the earth, churning the rock to liquid lava. To balance the heat of the fire sprites, water sprites dripped from heaven to people the seas and the rivers.

And in all of this, Faeja was pleased. He descended to the thread of time and walked beside His children on their earth, critiquing the beings they had created, the crudeness of their minds and the simplicity of their motivations.

Imagination again lifted the Lyre and struck up his former tune, gracing earth with all its beasts. But each new creation still fell short of Faeja's desires. Tired for a time, Imagination yielded up the Lyre to his sister Love. Love played a new song, imparting feeling for the first time into the ordered music of her brothers. From her notes came the merpeople, the first race of the new earth. The merpeople were a deeply passionate race, driven by emotion before thought. Their lives were as wild as the waves of the oceans they swam in, consumed by every feeling both light and dark.

After Love had finished, Endurance stepped to the Lyre. A perpetually silent deity, Endurance was the last Trait that any might have imagined creating. But Endurance had grown sick with watching the merpeople, disgusted by their inconstancy and subjugation to feeling. So, he played his own tune, a slow, haunting melody that clung to every note till the final echoes had faded. And from his song came the minotaurs. A hardy race, they stepped forth from the rock of the mountains and peopled the land left open by the merpeople.

Then, when the final notes of Endurance's long dirge had faded, Curiosity once again lifted the Lyre. And he made man, a race to balance the passion of the merpeople and the strength of the minotaurs. Gifted with both high reason and deep passion, man was driven by an insatiable need for knowledge.

After the creation of man, all of the Passions and the Traits began to understand the nature of creation and its new inhabitants. Many cried out for the Lyre. Philia created the elves, a tribal race bound by familial affection. Introversion created the dwarves, a race given to solitude and art.

In time, each of these races began to flourish, to grow and to multiply, taught and reared by the Passions and Traits they most admired. The Passions and the Traits became gods—rulers of races and dispensers of law. The world blossomed under the ever-flowing music of creation.

However, the Passions and the Traits were not perfect beings. Though modeled after the perfections of Faeja, their natures were subject to corruption; and experience altered their forms, letting their purity fall into distortion and entropy.

Malice, twisted by his association with Desire, grew tired of the simple, pastoral world which his brothers and sisters had created and crafted two new races: the eelings and the goblins. Beings of hatred and violence, these new races ravaged the rest of creation with the invention of war.

Grieved at the violence of His children, Faeja repented His gift of the Lyre and drew it back to himself. He sealed up the music of creation and bound His children within it, cutting them off from all reality outside of matter.

After the banishment, the peoples of the earth all but forgot Faeja and the time when He walked among them. The Passions and the Traits became lawless, struggling for dominance to fill the void left by Faeja. Their created races became armies in battles for lordship, and the Passions and the Traits became contenders in a battle for godhood.

Despite the removal of the Lyre, cyntras flowed freely through all of creation in the centuries following the banishment, leftover melodies from the first songs. Directionless, this power sparked creation wherever emotion reached climax. In battlefields and weddings, new creations sprang forth. Whenever a being felt an emotion in perfect sync with that emotion's Passion, whenever a being developed a trait in perfect sync with that Trait itself, cyntras became a usable power.

In all this time, the Passions and the Traits struggled for dominance, maneuvering the peoples of creation like pawns on a chessboard, toppling nations for personal grievances. It was not until the day of the first extinction that these minor deities finally repented of their struggles. The stories vary on what race died, but the scholars tell us that on that day Grief became the most powerful Passion the world had ever seen. So many tears fell, both of the Passions and of the peoples, that Grief harnessed the full cyntras of creation. Full of anguish and righteous indignation, Grief used his newfound power to bind all of the most powerful Passions and Traits in prisons beneath the earth, protecting creation from their lust.

Grief established a covenant with his remaining brothers and sisters to never again reign in the affairs of their creation. He guided the many peoples to a rich and fertile land he called Rehavan and left them there to carve their history.

Prologue

A strange hush hung over the festive nighttime streets of Candeline. The circus had come, and gaiety reigned in the tiny village. Above the peeling paint of the carts and the glorious moth-eaten stripes of the great circus tents, flickering candles dripped their tallow and wax in the dust of Candeline's streets. A single clown wandered these streets carrying a candlesnuffer on the tip of a long pole. He was a gnome, dressed in a grotesque approximation of a human Guard member, his wide, leathery features framed by a cerulean hood. He whistled as he walked the otherwise silent streets, shuffling in a peculiar, exuberant little dance. He spun a quick circle around his planted snuffer and then shot it out from his arm, neatly snuffing a candle that hung from a nearby pole.

Pastry crumbs and bones from fresh-fried fowl littered the dusty road, remnants of the evening's festivities. The gnome picked his way over them carefully, still dancing to his own music. It was his favorite time of the circus. His act was over, all of the other performers were sleeping in their beds, and he had the streets to himself, free from his identity as a mere entertainer, free from the laughter and gawking of the audience, many of whom had never before seen a gnome. The people of the village were all gathered together in the big tent, hundreds of silent farmers and miners listening in rapt attention to the circus's most-valued performer: the story-man.

No one knew how old the story-man really was. His withered, dried-apple face had seemed ancient when the gnome first joined the circus as a child. The story-man had no name or history, just his self-ascribed title—but he knew things, things old and beautiful and strange that no one could know, stories lost in the folds of time's cloak or buried in the vaults of death. Some said that he had sold his soul to Ingway for longevity and knowledge. Others that he was immortal. The gnome believed none of these things, but he still spread the rumors. They were good for business. He shot out his snuffer again and neatly extinguished a flame. He would stop thinking about the story-man now, about the circus. It was his time, the time when he was more than just a living novelty. He whistled and danced on down the streets as they darkened beneath his snuffer.

Under the canopy of the big tent, the story-man sat on a small stool in the center of a dimly lit stage. Spreading before him, a sea of faces stared upward, waiting for the coming tale. His hands spoke as much as his mouth as he began, flowing in rhythms that swelled and subdued the expanse of his tale, that dulled his sharper inflections to render them palatable and heightened his monotones with emotion.

"Tonight, we begin a tale nearly as old as the Iris of the human empire, a tale that was ancient when the hills around you had never felt the cut of a plow.

"All of you have heard the name of Reheuel, a name so steeped in legend that the stories obscure the man who lived them. The youngest child beneath this canvas tent could tell me the deeds of Reheuel's descendants, that favored family of immortals. But I wonder how many could tell me aught of the man behind the family.

"We honor Reheuel because he was the first immortal, because his descendants so faithfully served the Iris of the empire, forming the Guards, the Keepers, and the Healers. But I wonder if any of us pause to ask whether the man would crave this reverence, a man who denounced the empire for imperialism.

"Tonight, I wish to reach back to a time before the Hunter Wars had ended the reign of the immortals, to a time when the Iris of the human empire was still fresh and young. For that is the time when the immortal bloodline was first born, when Reheuel first entered the pages of history, pages he would then frequent for so very long.

"In this distant year, Reheuel dwelt as Captain of the Guards in the small town of Gath Odrenoch, a settlement carved from the foothills of the Gath mountains . . ."

Chapter 1

A tiny, glowing figure cut a swirling arc across the surface of a still pond, her bare feet leaving a trail of tiny ringlets in her wake. In front of her, a dragonfly flitted, its translucent wings casting back a light wind that stirred the fairy's hair. She laughed and reached out, stroking the dragonfly's scaly body. It veered sharply and raced away, leaving the fairy to seek other mischief.

On a nearby hill, a young girl stifled a giggle as she watched. Her older brother laid a warning hand on her shoulder. "Shh! You'll frighten her."

The little girl nodded vigorously and sealed her lips, drawing comically hard lines over her round features.

Her brother glanced away over the hill and then whispered, "Look! You can see the city now. The sun is just high enough. Do you see it, Veil, that silver shape on the horizon?"

Veil's eyes sparkled. "I see it, Hefthon! I see it—the Fairy City!"

Her brother smiled. "Tell me what it looks like."

Veil thought for a moment and then said slowly, "It looks like—more."

* * *

"Dust is a sign of idleness," Tressa said, sweeping a feather-tipped wand over her husband's bookcase.

Reheuel coughed as his wife continued flicking dust about his study. "And dusting is a sign of avoiding more worthwhile occupations."

Geuel, Reheuel's oldest son, glanced up from the pages of a worn book. "Oh, Father, please don't."

Tressa shook her duster at her husband menacingly. "Cleanliness means gentility! And I shall not have my husband, the *newly appointed* Captain of the Guards, living like a withered scribe in a dusty cubbyhole."

"But he's nearly fifty," Geuel called from his seat near the window. "Pretty soon he will be a withered scribe."

Reheuel glanced at his son and raised an eyebrow. "Since when do you get off with such comments, rogue? I raised you better."

Geuel set aside the fencing manual he had been reading and shrugged. "Oh, I don't know. Maybe you've just been letting things slip in your old age."

Tressa nodded with a gently mocking smile. "It has been terrible, darling, seeing you fade these past few years."

Reheuel laughed and wrapped his arms around his wife, lifting her from the floor. He swung her around him in a tight circle, clutching her waist in his strong hands. "Fade? Do you call this fading?" He lowered her down softly till she hung over the floor in his arms and planted his lips on hers, laughing through his kisses.

She laughed also and hung in his arms, staring at his face. "Sure, you can hold me here, old man?" she whispered.

Geuel rolled his eyes. "And that's my queue. I'll be in the stables with Hefthon." He planted his hands on the window ledge and began to launch himself outside.

"Use the door!" his mother shouted after him. "We need to be dignified."

Geuel landed lightly in the grass outside and strode toward the stables, shivering slightly in the evening chill. He was tall, twenty-one with a narrow but athletic build and dark, curly hair that helped widen his otherwise narrow features. As he entered the stable, he heard his younger siblings, Hefthon and Veil, chattering to the horses. Geuel stroked the nose of his charger, Iridius, and watched his siblings as they brushed their horses' coats. "Where did you ride?" he asked Veil.

The little girl grinned with ill-concealed excitement as she recited dutifully, "Nowhere special, just around the farms north of town."

Geuel laughed. "Don't bother, Veil. Leave the lying to your brother. He's better suited to it."

Hefthon threw his brush at Geuel in mock anger. He was a blonde, burly youth, large at nineteen and still growing, with thick, heavy features and a wide, simple face. "Better suited! I only learned it from you. Mother says that you and deception are like mermaids and water. The first would die without the second, and the second would lose its charm without the first."

Geuel shook his head. "How far did you ride, *really*? You've been gone all day."

"To the edge of the blue hills—but no farther. I was careful."

"You know better, Hefthon. There have been sightings," Geuel said, unsurprised but angry.

"I just wanted her to see the City of Youth, just once while she's still of age. Father showed us both when we were younger. And besides, Daris saw one goblin. That's hardly sightings."

"There's never only one," Geuel replied. "Risk your life for a sight-seeing trip if you want, but don't risk your sister's. Are we clear?"

Hefthon nodded. "Yes."

"Good, then I guess Father needn't hear of this."

* * *

Reheuel sat beside his wife in his study, softly stroking her back and whispering in low tones, "The Emperor has recalled another unit of guards from each of the inner cities. I'll have to send Hadrid and his men out soon."

"But you're already stretched so thin," Tressa replied.

"I know that, and you know that. But what does that mean to a ruler a thousand miles away? He only cares for his borders. The Empire is expanding—rapidly. Through conquest and truce alike. Before long, all the civilized lands in Rehavan will lie in the shadow of the Golden Iris. With such gains at the borders, what do towns like Gath Odrenoch matter? He hardly thinks of the dangers still within his realm."

"And the goblins?"

"We don't even know if the rumors are true. As far as the scouts can tell, only six or seven have left the mountain."

"I wish we would have killed them when we had the chance," Tressa said, "when our forces were still full."

Reheuel sighed. "Yes, that's what we say now, but we were sick of fighting."

"I just pray that they don't come here," Tressa whispered.

"So do I, Love. So do I."

Tressa lifted her head from his chest and smiled. "Love—after twenty-two years of marriage, the word still thrills me."

He smiled at her. "Has it been that long? You still look like the bashful maiden of eighteen who swore to be mine."

"And you still look like the confident guardsman who wooed me with songs in the evenings."

"Where does time go?" Reheuel asked, staring at his calloused, beaten hand as it slid across his wife's shoulders.

"It goes to our hearts, Love. Our hearts eat time, and they turn it to memories. Time never returns because it's already used up."

They sat still for a while longer, lost in silent remembrance, thumbing idly through the great volumes of their memories, prying the covers of dusty books and pulling apart pages that had become stuck and stiff through disuse and time.

It seemed to Reheuel, as he sat there, that his wife fed his mind, that her presence cleared his thoughts. The silence and her presence together drove his mind back through memories which had remained untouched for many years. Little glimmers flashed in his focus, special moments which used to be precious but, long since, had faded into obscurity. Little smiles that had flitted over his wife's lips, occasional glints of light in her hair, words spoken in the stillness of a summer evening—all these things rushed over him. He remembered moments which he had sworn never to forget—and had forgotten. He remembered moments that he had striven to burn out of his mind—but never had. It was all there for the reading—his life. Fifty years. All he had to do was turn the pages.

Darkness crept over the old farm that night, sweeping away the sounds and sights of daylight and giving way to its own nocturnal symphonies: crickets sang in the marshes, an owl questioned the night, and a band of coyotes yapped in the forest, scrapping over some minor prize. Geuel and Hefthon sat in the living room, their voices rising and falling to the flicker of dim candles melting on the table.

"It was stupid. You should never have left alone. Think of Veil. She's a child," Geuel said.

"I know she's a child. That's why I took her," Hefthon replied. "Do you remember what it felt like—to see Elicathaliss as a child? There was a moment, a moment when your heart stopped beating and a shudder rippled through your blood, screaming that you were alive and that the world was still beautiful."

"Yes, I loved that trip," Geuel replied, "and I remember the thrill—but you can't endanger your sister's life for a thrill."

"Thrill! You call it a simple thrill? I saw the city today. I saw her as a man, and all I saw were buildings. I saw tear-shaped buildings that glinted in the sun. Oh, she was still beautiful . . . But she was *only* beautiful. The magic was gone. Veil saw more than beauty. Where I saw buildings shining in sunlight, she saw the glint of innocence and the spark of youth."

"It's just a place," Geuel replied, "just a part of the world."

"Does that make it any less fantastic?" Hefthon replied. "Even dreams are part of this world. But Elicathaliss is more than just a place. She's immortal childhood, a place where innocence and wonder never die. To be a child and to see eternal youth, the opportunity only lasts so long. I wanted her to have that while she still could. She's growing: soon, the Fairy City won't matter."

Geuel sighed. "I know it's important to you. Just don't ride beyond the farmland anymore. I've heard things—in town. It's not safe out there."

"Fine, it won't happen again."

They blew out the candles and returned to their rooms in silence.

* * *

Dawn broke over Gath Odrenoch the following morning, and across the countryside men dragged themselves free from the loving arms of sleep, leaving her for the cold of life. Over the foothills, in the mountains of Gath, goblin laborers laid down their tools and crept back to their dark caverns, replacing man in sleep's fickle embrace.

Reheuel rose from his bed lightly, gently smoothing the blankets back over the form of his sleeping wife. He walked to the window and inhaled, swelling his muscled chest and basking in the morning chill. When he reached the kitchen a few minutes later, he found his children preparing a meal. They paused as he walked to his chair and then resumed.

Sitting down, he turned to Geuel. "We need to repair the fence in the southern pasture this morning, before I head into the city."

Geuel nodded. "Yes, Sir. I'll prepare some planks."

A few hours later, Geuel and his father stood along the wooden fence line in the southern field of their farm, Geuel digging at the base of a snapped post, trying to pry it from the clinging earth. Reheuel sat across from him, widening the slots in a new post with his hunting knife. He was already dressed in his uniform, the folds of his cerulean robe spread out over the field grass around him. "So, Geuel," he asked, "how have your fencing instructions progressed?"

"Quite well," Geuel responded with a grunt, his arms straining as he edged the post up its first inch. "Master Kezeik says I should be able to test next month."

His father nodded with a light smile on his lips, glancing up only briefly from his work. "Excellent, you shall be an officer one day if you continue as you have. And your archery?"

Geuel released the shovel and responded as he dug his hands down into the earth around the post, seeking a hold. "Not so well, I'm afraid. Master Deni tells me that if I were a hunter I would do best to dig a grave with my bow."

His father laughed. "That's just Deni's way. I expect you to focus more on archery though. We must be versatile. Specialization is a luxury that the guards can no longer afford."

"Yes, Sir," Geuel replied. He waited a few seconds to see if his father would continue, then asked, "Will there be fighting soon?"

"Someone has been listening to barracks-room gossip," Reheuel replied, standing and lifting the new post. "We don't know. We know that the goblins have been venturing farther afield, getting bold. Several farmers have reported vandalized fences and missing cattle. But, as far as actual war goes, no one knows. We haven't had a conflict with the creatures in decades. I was younger than you the last time they attacked. Who knows how many are even left up there."

"Would we win—if there were a war I mean?" Geuel asked.

"I'm confident we could defeat them," his father replied, "but win? I'd hardly call it victory. We would leave blood and bodies on the field, neither of which we can afford right now. The Emperor is still calling for conscripts, and we're running out of soldiers. No one would win."

Geuel tossed aside the stump of the old post and waited for his father to slide the new one into place. "I guess we should hope for peace then," he said.

"Always," his father replied.

Chapter 2

Four months passed, and rumors settled. Nervous hearts beat slower. As summer reached its peak, Gath Odrenoch returned to its sleepy routine.

Reheuel lay on the crest of a hill, his head resting on his saddle. It was his second day of travel, and it felt good to just lie still for a bit. Around him, the wild bluebarrels, namesakes of the Blue Hills, blossomed and trembled in the breeze, their beautiful barrel traps trembling enticingly for passing butterflies and other prey.

Staring off at the horizon, Reheuel could just spy the hazy outline of Elicathaliss. "The City of Youth," he whispered as he let his eyes trace the tear-shaped buildings that hung, dribbled along the horizon across the lazy river Faeja. "Amazing, isn't it, that a sign of grief should represent the innocent race?"

Standing nearby, Geuel nodded. "We all know about the symbol, Father."

"Tell me about the Tear, Daddy. I want to hear," Veil cried.

Reheuel leaned back and gazed at the sky, letting his voice sink into a rhythmic tone of narrative, delighted to tell a favorite tale. "Once upon a time, in the earliest days of creation, when the magic cyntras of the Passions and the Traits still flowed through all of creation, man lived in little villages along the banks of the Faeja. And in just such a village there was born a girl named Ariel. She was a perfect child, more beautiful and pure than any other creature. They say that the birds went silent when she sang and covered their faces in the plumage of their wings when she passed.

"Ariel grew and developed in perfect tune with Innocence, absorbing the cyntras of that great Trait. And for many years it seemed that she would never be corrupted. One day, though, when Ariel was no older than you, Veil, she discovered grief. Her father was murdered by bandits in the forest.

"Terrified and alone, Ariel ran away and hid in the rushes of the Faeja. And there she wept. And in her tears, all of her innocence flowed out, expelled by hate and grief. The tears, though, still held the cyntras of Ariel's innocence. And they pooled and collected in the water, hardening into the gem we call Ariel's Tear.

"The gem was so full of Innocence's power that when Ariel lifted it, it transformed her into a new being, a beautiful fairy. And since that time, the Tear has ever remained Ariel's symbol, the symbol of the Fairy Queen."

Hefthon grinned. "I can't believe we're actually going to visit. It's been so long."

Veil, who had paused to pick a bunch of bluebarrels, glanced up at her father. "Do you know Ariel?" she asked.

"I suppose, as much as any man knows a fairy. I've visited her city many times, and we speak. I give her news of the Empire."

Veil's eyes sparkled. "Can children still become fairies?" she asked.

"Yes, my dear. Every so often in this world, a child is born who doesn't quite belong, a child too simple to survive its grief. Ariel takes those children and changes them, giving them eternal youth. That's where fairies come from."

"I want to be a fairy!" Veil cried.

Reheuel chuckled. "I'm sure you do. But I'm afraid you have too much of your mother's mind and your father's spirit for that. Some day you will be blessed to raise a family or to labor in some other way, to give back to your world."

Veil wrinkled her nose in disgust. "That's old! I want to be young. I don't want to get wrinkly and tired and droopy."

Reheuel laughed. "Are you calling me wrinkly and droopy?"

Veil giggled, sensing her father's playful mood. "Yep, daddy's old, like Kezeik's hound."

Reheuel rolled over and faced his daughter, staring up at her with wide eyes and drooping lids, imitating Kezeik's endearingly hideous pet. His daughter responded with gales of laughter before grabbing his hand and saying with sudden urgency, "Hurry, Daddy! We're all rested. Let's keep going."

As he rode beside his father a few minutes later, Geuel asked, "Why *are* we going to the Fairy City, Father?"

"This world was given wonders for a reason," Reheuel replied. "They remind us that life is more than dull, drab pain. I want to give Veil something beautiful before reality dashes her illusions."

"And the human empire has no wonders?" Geuel asked. "How can the world be dull when we stand beneath the fluttering Golden Iris?"

Reheuel smiled. "You're proud of Gath Odrenoch? Of its people?"

"I would die for my city. It is a mark of human virility and endurance. We carved Gath Odrenoch from the face of a mountain, raised it in the heart of the wilderness. It is a symbol of man's power—like the Iris itself."

"And what if one day the Iris is not so noble? Our human Empire is complex, subject to the whims of its rulers. Elicathaliss is simple. Immortal childhood, immortal innocence. It is a wonder that will never corrupt."

"The Iris stands for ideals, not men," Geuel replied. "I would take pride in it even if all humanity were evil."

"Then cling to your pride, son. Never let it go. But—not all will share it. I lost my faith in the Iris when the ego of its ruler drove him to conquer rather than protect. I no longer look to the Iris's ideals. I look to the beauty I find in the world."

Hefthon, who rode just behind Geuel, said then, "I would say that the ideals of the Iris are not always reflected by the actions of its leaders. Perhaps loyalty to the Iris allows for distaste toward its government."

Geuel laughed. "My thoughts exactly, little brother."

Late that night, the family stopped to rest in a stand of pine, spreading their canvas tents beneath a thick canopy of boughs. Reheuel lay in his tent beside Tressa, whispering quietly as they listened to the children in the other tent. "They sound happy."

Tressa smiled, her glinting teeth the only thing visible in the tent. "I only hope that Veil can still see the city as a child."

"She can," he replied. "She's never known grief or pain. The city was made for those like her."

"How far is it?" Tressa asked, shifting herself closer and hunching her shoulders against the cold night air.

"Less than two days. It's a little under a four-day ride."

"Good. As much as I love riding, I'm starting to miss my bed."

Reheuel laughed. "You're getting old, my love. There was a time when a simple journey like this would hardly have affected you."

Tressa smacked him. He laughed.

"Old? I married a man ten years my senior, and yet he calls me old. What I would not give, my Love, just to stop the world right here, to halt the clock and slip into eternity as we are now."

"A tempting thought," Reheuel said.

"Can you imagine it? To live as timeless and changeless as the Fairy City, the two of us like this with our children forever? Why must things change?"

"Because change brought us to where we are," Reheuel replied as he twirled her hair in his fingers, "because change gave us what we have now."

A twig snapped outside the tent, and Reheuel froze. He clamped his hand gently over his wife's mouth and watched through the crack of the tent flap. A harsh, guttural huff sounded beside the fire. He reached for his sword. "Stay here," he whispered as he rose.

Reheuel flung back the flap of his tent and leapt into the open. The light from his family's smoldering fire cast dim shadows across the camp site. A creature stood in the glow, green eyes glittering in the light. It was a small goblin, about four and a half feet tall, lithe and gangly like all its kind. Its freakishly long limbs bulged with sinewy, narrow muscles that seemed ready to burst through its tightly stretched skin. Its massive, flat nose steamed as it breathed in the darkness, and its long, spindly fingers clutched a sickle-shaped sword.

Reheuel yelled and swung his broadsword, arcing the blade at a downward angle toward the creature's neck. It dropped to all fours and sprinted for the trees, nickering in a series of eerie clicks. It leapt for a branch and swung into the pine trees, using the weight of its body like the head of a flail on the end of its slender limbs. Reheuel ran to the tents to check on his children. When he reached them, Hefthon was stumbling from the door, his spear clutched in his hands. Geuel stood at the other end of the tent, his sword low and ready. Veil sat in a ball in the middle, her blankets drawn over her head in fear.

"How many?" Geuel asked, his eyes flickering over the tree line.

"Only saw the one," Reheuel replied. "Probably drawn to the fire."

"What do we do?" Hefthon asked, his voice quavering with nerves and adrenaline.

Reheuel put up his sword. "Come out, Tressa," he called. "It's gone." He turned to his sons. "We're closer to Elicathaliss than to home. We'll keep riding."

Geuel nodded. "Hefthon, help me with the tent," he said. "Veil, gather the blankets."

Veil nodded. Wide-eyed, she began rolling up her blanket. Tressa embraced her and whispered assurance.

Reheuel walked back to the tree where the goblin had disappeared. About twenty feet up its trunk, he saw several gaunt forms cringing on its branches. He growled and slashed at the tree with his sword. The creatures leapt from their perches into nearby branches, and he heard them crashing away through the treetops. He spun about. "Leave the tents! Hefthon, the horses. Geuel, keep your spear ready. There are more."

Tressa stood, clutching Veil in her arms. "How many?"

"I don't know," Reheuel replied. "Just keep Veil close."

He cast several sticks on the fire, and the flame soon lit up the surrounding woods. Bright glints in several treetops betrayed the eyes of watching creatures. Within minutes, Reheuel and his family were riding away, tents still pitched in the forest. As he rode, Reheuel watched the treetops. Twice, he saw dim forms swinging from the branches. Once, a blade glinted in the moonlight. They broke the edge of the forest after about an hour's ride, and Reheuel stopped his horse to gaze back at the trees. He couldn't tell if the rustling was the wind, but many of the treetops swayed and rocked. He spun his horse and dug in his spurs. "We ride till morning," he said to his family. "Spare the horses though. I doubt they'll follow."

Tressa pulled her horse alongside his as they rode. "How many?" she asked.

"Many," he said. "After we reach the city, I'll return to Gath Odrenoch. If the goblins are coming down in force, they must be warned."

"Should we turn back?"

Reheuel shook his head. "Too dangerous. They're riled now. I wouldn't risk you and Veil."

Hours passed as they traveled. Night scattered in the rays of dawn. Dawn brightened to day, and finally night fell once more. They halted in the open this time, far from any trees or cover. Geuel and Reheuel took turns watching through the night.

They rode hard the next day, and, as they crested the brow of a hill in the afternoon, the glistening, tear-shaped spires of the Fairy City appeared, still distant on the plain below. Despite the terrors of the recent night and the weight of his new knowledge, Reheuel smiled as he saw the city.

Veil uttered a sharp cry at the sight of it. "It's beautiful!"

Hefthon laughed. "It is, indeed, Veil."

"What is it made of?" she asked, squinting at the silvery, glinting spires. It's so smooth."

"Thought, little one. It's made of thought," Reheuel replied. "The Fairies create for the beauty of creating. They weave their city with nothing but the power of Ariel's Tear and their own imagination. Whole cities blossom in the sky sometimes, hanging gardens and waterfalls of light suspended from the clouds."

Geuel sighed. "Such power, it's a wonder they don't spread over all the earth as they build."

"That's the beauty of youth," Reheuel said. "They don't build for vanity or power. Their creations fade as soon as their focus shifts. The central city stands by the power of

Ariel and the other rulers. But everything else fades with new creations. No wonder lasts forever."

"Such waste," said Geuel.

"Such beauty," said Hefthon.

Tressa shaded her eyes. "Is that—smoke?"

"Where?" Reheuel asked, tensing immediately.

"Over the city, to the left of the central spire."

Reheuel nodded. "It is—Hefthon, stay with your mother and sister. Ride after us slowly. Geuel, follow me!"

Reheuel dug in his spurs and took off, flashing across the hills in front of his family, Geuel close behind.

Foam spattered his horse's flanks and stained his breeches when he finally leapt from his horse's back, running instantly toward the gate of Elicathaliss. He could see the smoke clearly now, black plumes rising from the city's heart. Hundreds of fairies swarmed in the air, visible in every direction over the gate, spinning in circles, flashing to and fro like frightened children, screaming in confusion. The ringing of stone and steel echoed from within the city. The gate stood open several feet, and Reheuel ducked inside. Elicathaliss, despite the size of its tiny denizens, was built as if for men, and Reheuel navigated its shining streets with ease.

The city was a great maze of intersecting tunnels and fantastic arches. The walls were built of silver, but not the dull silver of reality, the silver of thought, silver as it appears in dreams. The ceiling glistened like diamond, splitting light into a thousand colors and reflecting them off specks of mirror that dotted the marble floor.

But Reheuel could not pause to admire the architecture as he ran. The sounds of fire and striking iron drew him down winding, labyrinthine hallways and over open causeways toward the city's center. Soon, he could hear the Faeja, the river over which the Fairy City arched, rushing beneath his feet.

Reheuel paused at a corner, drew his sword, and leaned for a moment against the wall. Geuel stopped beside him, panting slightly.

Reheuel patted his shoulder. "Around the next bend, there's a courtyard. If the keep hasn't fallen, that's where the fighting will be. When we go in, stay close. Don't take any risks. Understand?"

Geuel nodded. "I understand."

"The goblins are weaker in the sunlight. They can't see very well. But they're still dangerous. Ready?"

Geuel nodded. "Yes,"

Reheuel smiled. You make me proud." He turned the corner and stepped into the courtyard. It had been a crystal garden, filled with clear, hanging boxes of diamond vines and opal roses. Along the ground, sapphire-streaked, crystal Lady Slippers lay shattered and crushed amid swathes of bent golden irises.

In the center of the garden, a single silver tower stood twenty stories high, perfectly octagonal with a flat roof. Around its walls, about twenty goblins clambered, swinging wildly from ledge to ledge, scraping iron blades against chinks and joints, prying at the edges of windows, and shrieking in harsh, guttural monosyllables.

Reheuel approached behind two that stood at the main gate of the tower, swinging pickaxes at the silver door. He swung once, and the larger of the creatures fell. Before he could follow with a second blow, the other screeched and scrabbled up the side of the building, chattering to its fellows. Reheuel backed away from the tower, getting out of jumping range, and clutched Geuel's jacket. "Don't get any closer. Let them come to us."

The goblins on the walls hissed and spat, nickering in confused anger. They pushed themselves out from the wall periodically and strained at their handholds, as if searching for an opportunity to pounce.

"Get any closer and they'll swarm us," Reheuel said. "Keep your distance."

Suddenly a sharp cracking sound came from the far side of the building about fifteen feet up as one of the farther creatures penetrated a window. The others spun about and scrabbled along the wall toward the far side, anxious to enter.

"The door! Get to the door!" Reheuel cried.

Geuel sprinted for the door and struck it with his fist. "Open up!" he cried. "We'll help you!"

Shrieks and screams echoed from inside, mixed with the chunnering laughter of the goblins. Through dozens of tiny holes in the wall, openings no larger than a fist, hundreds of fairies came flying in fear. Many were bleeding, their lights dull and flickering. Flakes of wing drifted around them like leaves, torn on the silver walls.

Reheuel pounded at the door beside his son. "Please! Ariel! Open the door!"

Suddenly the door slid open, vanishing into the walls of the tower like folded blades. Reheuel grabbed his son's shirt. "Follow me. The throne room."

They entered and found themselves in a massive, round hall. Its domed ceiling, painted in a mural of the night sky, hung a distant forty feet above them. Along each side of the outer wall, staircases wound in semicircles, linking the hall to the higher floors. Reheuel ran to the nearest and leapt up the stone steps, coughing with the exertion of the last hours.

Geuel shadowed him, sword still drawn, staring at the gore that spattered the floors and stairs. He stopped and nearly hurled when he saw a female leg lying on the steps in front of him, its entirety no longer than his smallest finger. Aside from a few specks of blood, smaller than raindrops to a human, it looked—clean—garishly whole and undefiled.

At the top of the steps, Reheuel paused to clear his breathing. Then he ran through the door, his empty sheath flapping against the silver walls, gouging the floral filigree with its brass cap. "Two halls further on the right," he called over his shoulder. "Innocence spare them! I hope we're not too late."

Geuel nodded and hurried to catch up, ashamed at falling behind.

A few minutes later, they turned and entered a kind of entry hall before a large open archway. In the archway, tendrils of a solid light spun and cavorted, weaving themselves together into ropes and wicker walls. Eight goblins stood in the doorway, hacking at the trails of light and tearing them apart, casting them aside as they strove to break through the growing barrier. The broken tendrils dissipated as they struck the floor. Countless fairies lay dead before the door, their mangled bodies dwarfed by three goblin corpses.

Geuel drew his dagger in his left hand and looked to his father.

"Don't hesitate," Reheuel said and lunged forward at the distracted goblins. He swung twice before they could react, leaving one dead and another mildly injured. Geuel caught one of the stragglers in the hamstring and left it writhing.

The others spun around and gnashed their spindly teeth in anger, snarling and snorting through their broad noses. One charged, waving a wooden mallet embedded with nails. Reheuel caught its swing on his sword, and his son ran it through.

Three more ran forward lowering spears, and Reheuel and Geuel backed into the narrower hallway. As they entered, Geuel gasped. "The lights!" he cried.

Reheuel looked back to the archway and saw the lights begin to fade, withering like living tissue. "They're weakening," he said. "We have to get into the throne room." He moved forward and swung at one of the spears, turning it aside. Stepping past the goblin's guard, he swung downward and split its crown. Geuel hurled his dagger at another, distracting it long enough for him to leap past its spear and pierce its chest. The third dropped its spear and ran after its fellows, chattering wildly as it entered the throne room.

Reheuel ran after it and skidded on a slick of blood, sliding into the throne room off balance. About chest level in the room, a circle of nine fairies hovered, facing outward. Their translucent wings flashed wildly in a haze of scarlet, silver, and cerulean light. Around them, tendrils of solid light flickered and spun, winding like the tentacles of some dying beast, knocking aside the goblins that edged in too close. In the center of the circle, a female fairy with black hair and a scarlet dress hovered clasping a tear-shaped gem the size of her body.

Reheuel swung his sword at one of the goblins closest to the door, but it ducked and skittered across the stone floor to the far side of the fairy ring, nickering wildly.

"They hardly notice us," Geuel said, swinging at a second creature.

It caught his blade in the crook of a sickle and knocked it aside before running back at the circle of fairies, leaping high in the air, long arms extended for a blow.

"They're after the fairies," Reheuel said.

He swung once more and caught the goblin he had wounded earlier in the side. It collapsed to the stone floor with a click of bony joints.

Just then the tendrils of light around the fairy circle shattered and fell to the ground. A goblin snickered as it flicked a lightless fairy from its spear tip. The other goblins leapt in toward the ring and sent its members scattering.

The central fairy dropped her gem as a blow from a goblin's palm sent her flying toward the wall.

"Ariel!" Reheuel cried and leapt to catch her, dropping his sword. Geuel stepped forward and crouched protectively over his body.

Three of the goblins turned and closed in, eyes squinting in the light from the window, faces flecked with spittle and blood. The fourth, clutching Ariel's gem, scrambled over the windowsill.

Geuel swung out tentatively, tapping aside the tip of the nearest goblin's sword. It recoiled and then crept back. They were bent low, crawling, their knees popped high over their backs and elbows tugging them along the floor. Their heaving, bony chests scraped against the floor, and their sickles hung loosely beside them. Geuel slowly backed up, scattering chips of silver stone as he slashed the floor in front of their faces.

Reheuel stood behind him. "I can't get to my sword," he said.

Without turning, Geuel handed him his dagger, and together they stood facing the remaining creatures. One sprang suddenly at Reheuel, launching itself from its coiled rear legs like a frog. Reheuel stepped back and caught its blade on the dagger but tripped on a body. The goblin straddled his chest.

Geuel tried to turn, but the remaining goblins cut him off, chattering in nickers and clicks, their eyes glinting with a devilish amusement. Geuel stepped forward and thrust twice, both times striking air as the goblins snaked around his blade, weaving with an offhand ease. He kicked at one, causing it to leap back, and then charged its fellow, swinging low and wide. It caught his blade, but he slid his sword back from its parry and thrust under the raised sickle, piercing it under the collar bone. He kicked it off his blade and turned back toward the second.

Reheuel lay on his back, his dagger held at an angle, its curved guard locked with the guard of the goblin's knife, barely holding the blade away from his throat. He grunted as he felt his arms slowly giving way.

The goblin's eyes strained and bulged in their sockets, and its temples throbbed as it strained with all its sinewy might to finish the blow.

Just as the blade touched Reheuel's neck, a flash of red light cut across his vision and struck the goblin's neck, knocking it off balance. It grabbed wildly at its throat, but Ariel held on and thrust again and again with her tiny, pin-like dagger, rupturing the goblin's artery and finally snapping her blade on its tough skin. A spray of blood drenched the Fairy Queen as the goblin slid to the ground, gurgling confusedly and clutching its throat.

Reheuel turned and saw his son facing the last creature and approached it from behind. Grasping its head in his knotty hands, he jerked tightly and snapped its neck.

"Pretty good for an old man," Geuel said with a laugh.

Reheuel snorted and grabbed his sword from the ground. "Let's see you do it."

He turned away and looked for Ariel. She knelt in a nearby corner, cradling the head of another fairy in her lap. Her entire right side still dripped with blood, staining her marble skin and scarlet dress. "They're gone, Randiriel," she whispered. "It's over."

The other fairy, a blonde female in a green, blood-shot dress, trembled and wept like a child. "They'll be back, they'll be back . . ." she repeated in a rhythmic monotone, staring at the archway with hollow eyes.

Ariel sighed and rocked her for a few more seconds, whispering into her ear. Then she lowered her softly to the floor and turned back to Reheuel, flitting up to his level.

Reheuel nodded to the goblin she had killed. "Youthful innocence?" he asked.

"Not all of us have such a blessing," Ariel replied.

Reheuel glanced at the remaining fairies from the ring of nine. "And them?"

"There were nine of us," Ariel said, "nine elders who gave up youth to lead the others. We were the strongest and the oldest."

Reheuel pointed to the fairy in the corner. "She all right?" he asked.

Ariel shook her head. "Randiriel wasn't an elder. She stayed to fight, even in her innocence. It's never happened before."

"I'm sorry," Reheuel said. He began to turn away. "We saw more outside. We'll find them."

Ariel shook her head. "They're gone. They have what they came for. I can feel my city, and she is clean."

Chapter 3

Hefthon stood at the gates of the fairy city, nervously sliding his sweaty hand along the grip of his spear, tightening his palm around the leather thongs that wound its shaft. "I should go in," he said.

"Wait for your father," Tressa said. "It's not safe here for Veil."

"He could need me," Hefthon snapped. "There hasn't been a sound since he went in."

"He could need you," his mother replied. "But Veil *does* need you. Restrain yourself."

Hefthon jabbed the butt of his spear into the earth and sank to his haunches. "You're right, I'm sorry."

"She's always right, Hefthon. One of the first lessons I learned after wedding her."

Hefthon glanced up and saw his father and Geuel approaching the gate, just turned from a side street. Hefthon leapt to his feet. "What is it? Goblins? Is the city lost?" he asked.

Reheuel clapped him on the shoulder. "No, she is not lost, though there are many dead. They've taken Ariel's Tear as well."

Hefthon tore his spear from the earth. "We have to pursue them," he said.

Reheuel shook his head. "*We* don't have to do anything. You and Geuel will stay here with Veil and your mother."

Tressa looked up quickly. "Reh," she said, "what are you thinking? Reh? Look at me."

Reheuel sighed. "I can't let them take it, Tressa. Without that tear, this city won't last the month. It'll fade. It's only standing now by the power of a few exhausted fairies. If they don't get the Tear back, the world will lose another wonder."

"You don't know how many there are."

Reheuel whistled for his horse which stood grazing a few yards off.

"Reh, look at me. You're not twenty. Wait till you can get your men."

Reheuel shook his head. "There's no time. I have to stop them before they reach the mountains."

Geuel took the bow and quiver from his horse. "Father," he said, holding them out. "You'll need these more than I."

"String?"

"In the pouch on the side of the quiver. Good luck."

Reheuel strapped the bow into place on his own horse. "Thank you, son. Take care of our family. Lock down the gates and barricade yourself with the fairies. If I'm not back in two days, head for Gath Odrenoch. I'll meet you there."

Veil ran forward and clasped him around the waist. "Don't go," she begged.

Reheuel dropped down to his knees and grabbed his daughter by the shoulders. "I know you're afraid, Love. But I have to go. There are people who need my help. What have I told you about help, Veil?"

"The stronger are gifted for the weaker," Veil recited, tears running down her cheeks.

Reheuel smiled. "That's right, my Passion. And right now, there are a great many of the weak who need my help. What is strength?"

"Selflessness," Veil answered quietly, sniffing back her tears.

"Be strong, Veil," Reheuel whispered.

He stood and kissed his wife on the lips. "I'll be back," he said. Then he leapt on his horse and turned it to the north, tapping his spurs against its flanks.

* * *

"We should go inside," Geuel said. He extended his arm to Tressa. "Come, Mother." He smiled. "I'm sure he'll be safe."

Hefthon gathered the reins of the remaining horses and followed behind, staring at the scars of the Fairy City as they walked.

Geuel led his family away from the city's keep, carefully avoiding the center of the battle. But still, tiny bodies occasionally littered their path. Veil trembled as she passed them, unable to pull her eyes away from the pitiful remains. After he had found a building to stay in, Geuel turned to his brother. "Stay with them. I'm going to lock down the gates."

Hefthon nodded.

"And brother? Keep them out of the streets," Geuel said. "There are things they shouldn't see."

As he walked to the main gate, Geuel heard a fluttering behind him and turned. Ariel was flying toward him, washed now and clean of blood.

"Did Reheuel pursue them?" she asked.

"He did," Geuel answered. "You knew he would."

"You think he is wrong?" Ariel asked.

"It's your problem," Geuel replied. "I'm sorry for your pain, but he owes you nothing."

"So, men have no stake in our affairs?"

Geuel began walking again. "Only the stake they impose on themselves."

"And have you seen no beauty here worth saving?" Ariel asked.

"None worth my father's blood."

"You have changed," Ariel said sadly. "As a child, you were so full. You are not merely older, you are—lesser, harder."

"When we met, I was a child."

"You're right," Ariel said. "Your family owes me nothing. But you have done my people great service today. And if your father succeeds, I will grant your family the greatest gift that mankind has ever known . . . Consider that your stake." She turned and carved a path back toward the keep, her red streak dimmer than usual.

After he had closed the gates, Geuel headed for the keep, planning to clean away the traces of battle before Veil and Tressa had to see them. He entered the main door and paused beside the stairs. Three fairies, including Ariel, were picking their way across the hall, dragging twig biers to remove their dead. It was an oddly pathetic sight, three winged beings of ethereal beauty trapped on the ground dragging carnage.

Geuel removed his leather vest and lay it beside the stairs. Carefully, he began gathering little corpses from the silver floor and laying them on his vest. The bodies felt even frailer than they looked, like broken sparrows. He constantly feared that he would break one.

Ariel cast him a sad smile of thanks as she worked.

On the stairs, the green-dressed fairy Randiriel sat shaking one of the bodies. "Maeva? Maeva?" she whispered. "It's time to wake up."

The body she shook was torn in the middle, nearly halved. Only the spine and a few threads of flesh still connected its abdomen.

Geuel stared for a few seconds. "Can't you—do something?" he asked Ariel. "She's going mad."

"With the Tear, maybe," Ariel replied, lowering the bier she dragged and glancing back at Randiriel. "I could try to heal her. There's nothing now though. The Tear was a link. It united our thoughts and emotions. Without it, each fairy is alone—many for the first time that they can remember."

Despite the number of bodies, it took Geuel and the council members only an hour or so to gather them all together. They made a pathetically small pile—scores upon scores of bodies and still not enough to fill a coffin. Even with the nine goblins, the physical remains painted a poor picture of the battle's true cost.

As Geuel deposited the last of the bodies in an empty building behind the keep, Ariel landed beside him. "Go back to your family," she said. "We can clean the blood."

Geuel nodded. "I'm sorry, Ariel," he whispered, visibly shaken. He stared at the mangled little corpses on the floor. Most still had their eyes open—and those tiny eyes, animal in size but otherwise all too human, sent a chill down his spine. "Perhaps—perhaps my father was right."

A few minutes later, Geuel entered the archway of the house where his family was staying.

"Any news?" Hefthon asked.

"Nothing new," he replied.

"Are you hurt?" Veil asked, drawing closer and pointing to his bloodstained hands.

Geuel glanced down and saw the drying red stains that ran up his wrists and spread across the undersides of his sleeves. He resisted the urge to thrust them behind his back and began backing toward the door. "No, no, I'm fine, Veil. Just excuse me for a moment."

He left and drifted toward the main gate. There were troughs there, channels carved to allow water from the Faeja to run out through the portions of the city that rested on solid earth. He could wash there. When he reached the gate, he paused and studied the walls. They looked different than they had in the morning, duller, like silver coins after years of use. The gems hardly reflected the sunlight. He shook himself, assuming that he was fatigued.

* * *

"Whoa, Etteni," Reheuel said, drawing his horse to a halt on the edge of a dense pine forest. He eyed the trees distrustfully, studying the boughs for movement. The goblins would gain time in the forest. Their slender, agile builds allowed them to move more quickly swinging through the trees than traveling on the ground. But he still hesitated to follow, knowing that he would be vulnerable beneath the branches.

He nudged his horse forward into a gentle walk, constantly scanning the boughs overhead as he rode. Occasionally, he saw the white of freshly broken branches where a swinging goblin had misjudged its hold. He pulled open his water skin and took a quick pull, knowing he would need to be fresh if it came to hard riding.

He rode for several miles, occasionally pausing to listen for movement. But no sound ever greeted him. Eventually he pushed his horse to a heavy canter, still staring upward, constantly searching for movement in the trees.

Night fell as he exited the forest. The trees had slowed him, and he knew that the goblins would keep moving through the night. But they would be tired, perhaps more tired than he was after their long trek to the city.

He patted Etteni's neck. "Sorry, girl, can't let you stop tonight." Hours passed as he rode, constantly sighting himself with the distant peak of Ondurin. As long as he kept himself in line with the peak, he could forego tracking. He knew where the goblins were heading.

The grim outline of the mountain, silver-edged in the light of a half-moon, stirred his memories of the old war, the battle to build Gath Odrenoch. The builders had begun with the walls first, carting in old pines from the feet of the mountain and sinking them, entire, as posts. The cart drivers carried crossbows beneath their seats, often drawn and bolted. The laborers never shed their swords.

For months, the goblins had made their little salvos, taking a lone laborer who wandered too far from his group, a stray goat from the pastures. And then, the very night that the wall was completed, they had attacked, crawling over the walls in the darkness while the elated men slept off an evening of revelry.

Dozens had died.

Reheuel could still remember the weeping, the screams of the wounded, the cold of the rain in the morning as he marched with the laborers, the cut of the shale as he slid down gorges with his ax strapped to his back and his spear in his hands.

They had reached the goblin city in the daylight, and they had stormed it. No plan, no leader, just angry husbands and sons and fathers—eager for blood. It was a miracle that most survived, a greater miracle that they won. Reheuel counted in his mind the cost of that battle: his brother, his uncle, his cousins—forty-seven laborers and twenty guards in all. Gath Odrenoch had never been the same after. It had grown, blossomed even with a new generation rising to take the place of the fallen. But its founders still remembered. They dwelt on blood-stained ground.

"Should have killed them when we had the chance," Reheuel whispered to his horse, "should have followed them from their city and down into the caves, slaughtered every last one of them."

Etteni snorted.

"Suppose you're right," Reheuel said with a chuckle. "Just big talk from an old soldier. Nobody wanted to dig more graves."

Reheuel's thoughts ran back. He stood, his arms running with scarlet-tinted rain and his chest heaving, staring into the mouth of the goblin caves. As far as he could see, there was only darkness, interspersed with crevices and alcoves in the rock. "We should follow," he said, pulling his wet hair from his eyes.

The Captain shook his head from where he lay nearby. He spat out the end of a bandage he had been tying with his teeth. "They're gone, and they won't come back down the mountain. We're done here."

Reheuel turned back from the cave. "For now," he said under his breath.

Etteni suddenly reared back and whinnied, nearly sending Reheuel to the ground. "Easy, girl!" he said, grasping tightly to the pommel. "What's the matter?"

As if to answer, a guttural snarl sounded from the darkness and an arrow struck Reheuel's scabbard, shattering on the steel beneath the leather.

Reheuel turned back his heels and pricked his spurs against Etteni's flank. "Ride!" he shouted.

Etteni took off in fear, nostrils filled with the scent of goblins and their half-tanned raw-hide clothing. She cut a forty-five-degree angle, veering away from the source of the arrow. And, after a few seconds, howling chatter filled the air from every side.

Reheuel drew his sword and hugged close to Etteni's back, struggling to find a target in the night. But the moon had shielded herself in cloud, and only blurred shadows moved in the darkness. A sharp sting in Reheuel's thigh told him he'd been hit. The next moment, Etteni crashed forward to her chest, flinging Reheuel over her head to the ground. He rolled to a stop and scrabbled backward to grab his weapon, disoriented and half-blind.

As he grasped the handle of his sword, the edge of a cloud bank slid off the moon and Reheuel saw his enemies. There were only a handful—four, maybe five. All on the far side of his horse. Lifting the sword, he ran to the side of the beast and crouched down beside it. "Sorry, old friend," he whispered, staring at the arrows embedded in its neck and side.

A hiss caused him to flatten, and another arrow buried itself in the flesh of his mount. Forcing himself tightly against the beast's side, Reheuel felt a trail of horse blood run down into the back of his shirt. He shuddered at the warm wetness on his spine. An arrow struck the grass beside his foot, causing him to quickly tuck it in. He could hear claws now, scraping the earth on the far side of the horse, easing hesitantly forward with staggered, hungry rushes. Th goblins were circling, looking for a clear shot. He slid off his cloak and waited.

After a few seconds, he heard the goblin farthest to his right edge in closer. Too close. He slung his coat out to the left, hoping to draw their fire. Then he ran to the right, screaming inarticulately and trying to ignore the searing pain in his thigh where a snapped shaft tugged at his cotton pants.

He reached the goblin just as it notched a second arrow. Grabbing it by the throat, he spun in a circle and crouched behind its gangly body. Two arrows struck its back, and a third buried itself in the grass at his feet. He slung the corpse aside and ran forward. Two goblins dropped their bows and pulled out sickle-shaped swords, gnashing their teeth on the blades threateningly. The third nocked another arrow.

Reheuel ignored the third and ran between the first two, trying to obscure any shot. Instantly, they closed in, snaking out their long arms and trying to hook his ankles with their blades. Bent almost double to stay at their level, Reheuel batted at their blades and tried to keep them at a distance. Seeing an opening, he then leapt forward and swung downward at the nearest, burying his sword in the sinews of its neck. He quickly knelt and lifted its sickle, no larger than a dagger in his hand, and spun around. Ten yards—two full rotations. He let the sickle fly. An arrow shot wildly to Reheuel's left as the goblin with the bow staggered backwards.

As Reheuel stood, the last goblin swung, wrapping its sickle around his side. He felt the point strike his back and enter above his kidney. He staggered forward with the force of the blow and grabbed the sickle's handle. The goblin tugged at it frantically, struggling to finish the blow. Reheuel lowered the tip of his sword to its forehead. "Where are the others?" he asked.

The goblin released the sickle, leaving it hanging, curled around Reheuel's back like a grotesque belt. It tensed to jump backward, and Reheuel jabbed its forehead, drawing a spurt of blood. "Ah!" he said.

It shuddered and leered angrily. "With the gem," it said, sputtering and clicking over the words as if finding the common tongue distasteful.

"Where?"

The goblin began edging away, and Reheuel prodded it once more. "Where?"

"We said we'd signal when we finished you." It snickered. "Haven't had a full meal in days."

"Signal," Reheuel said, gently burrowing his sword tip into its forehead.

The goblin shook its head, and Reheuel kicked its knee, snapping it. "Signal."

The goblin shrieked from the ground and pulled a horn from its side, quickly blowing three notes.

"Is that it?" Reheuel asked.

The creature nodded. "Free?" it asked, trembling.

"Perhaps on a better night."

Chapter 4

Veil sat up slowly from her blankets, careful not to wake Tressa who lay beside her. Her mother's cheeks were gray, furrowed by the tears she had let fall while Veil slept. A staggered series of light columns filtered through the gems set in the thin wall, casting blue and red specks of light on the floor. Veil walked to the door and stared out into the street. The walls looked duller than they had the night before, dry like aged bones. A tiny green figure flitted by along the street and entered a nearby building. Veil followed curiously.

As she entered the building, she heard a light hum. The fairy in the green dress hovered near the center of the room, eyes closed and fists clenched. All about the room, silver laces, golden weaving, and crystal flowers floated trembling in the air, glowing just brighter than the room itself. Veil smiled. "What are you doing?" she asked.

"The others are letting things fade," the fairy said, "even the things that have always been. I can't let it happen. I don't want them to fade—like Maeva."

Veil lifted one of the crystal flowers, spinning it gently in her fingers. "Did you make these?" she asked.

"Yes. I used to have thousands."

Veil sniffed the flower. It smelled of stone dust and jasmine. "Father said that fairies never kept what they made."

"They don't," the fairy said. She glanced around. "I used to hide them here. I would come and sit and admire them when I was alone. The others wouldn't like it, wouldn't understand."

"Well, I think they're beautiful," Veil said, setting the flower back down. "I'm Veil. What's your name?"

"Randiriel," the fairy replied. "But you can call me Rand."

"Are you alone?" Veil asked. "I haven't seen any others here."

"The others are hiding," Randiriel said sadly. "Ariel and the council have gathered them in the tower. They're scared . . . Bad things happened."

Veil frowned. "Father said the fairies needed help."

"Yes, we are alone. We—I—" she seemed to struggle with the word. "I've never been alone before. The Tear was all of us."

"What will happen without the Tear?" Veil asked.

"The flowers broke," Randiriel replied distractedly. "All the flowers broke."

"The city's getting dimmer," Veil said.

"The Tear was all of us, and we are the city."

"You sound old," Veil said. "Father said that the fairies were children."

Randiriel smiled sadly. "We're alone now. But I've always been different." She pointed to the flowers. "The others let them fade."

Veil nodded and backed toward the door. "I won't tell," she said as she left.

* * *

Hefthon stood in Elicathaliss's keep. The building was clean now, scrubbed free of gore and blood, sprinkled with water scented by wildflowers. Over a thousand fairies flitted to and fro in the main hall and huddled in masses in the little alcoves and ridges and chairs that covered the walls, tiny ledges to the human eye but balconies as large as rooms to the fairies.

Ariel stood on Hefthon's shoulder, gesturing to the trembling innocents. "They're broken," she said, her voice holding the tears she could never shed. "They're broken, and I can't fix them."

Hefthon sighed. "You're doing what you can. Father will bring the Tear."

"It wasn't meant to be like this," Ariel said. "They were meant to be protected—eternal."

Hefthon reached a hand as if to offer comfort and then realized the foolishness of the gesture. "You did your best. This place has been a haven longer than the oldest race can remember."

Ariel sat down. "Life is bitter," she said slowly. "It is cold and cruel and full of hurt. I thought I could give them something else, some beautiful little corner where time was cheated." She gestured to all her sisters and brothers. "They were the weak, the soft, and the gentle. I was supposed to keep them pure."

"You did," Hefthon replied. "And you kept the world that much purer as well."

Ariel ran her fingers through her dark hair. "But what is a thousand years in this world? The space between a smile and a tear? I meant to give them eternity, just one beautiful constant in this changing world . . . But I was weak."

"Perhaps you don't need to be strong," Hefthon replied. "I love this place as well. More than all the glory of the human empire. I cannot promise you eternity, but I can promise you that should Father succeed, for as long as I live, I will protect this city."

Ariel looked up at his face. "For as long as you live?" she asked.

"Yes."

* * *

Geuel woke late. His back lay propped against the wall facing his building's main archway. He stared for a few seconds, accustoming himself to his surroundings. A light breeze sang in the withered crystal blossoms outside the door. The city looked dull and sickly, the silver buried beneath a gray hue, closer to lead. He picked at the wall at his back and felt it flake off in slivers under his nail.

Tressa stood nearby at a fake counter, spreading honey onto some bread. She smiled. "Morning, son. The others are outside already."

"Did you tell Veil to stay close?"

"She's in the building across the street," Tressa said. "I think Hefthon headed for the keep."

"Hope his stomach's empty," Geuel muttered.

"Pardon?" Tressa asked.

"Nothing," he said. "I'll tell Veil there's food."

"Thank you."

Geuel walked out into the street. "Veil?" he called.

Silence. He walked into the building across the way and stopped. Crystal flowers and sculptures levitated around the room, glowing brightly in the dimmed surroundings, the only objects lit by the Fairy City's usual dreamlike brightness. In the center of the room, the green-dressed fairy floated in the air, shuddering violently with exertion.

"Randiriel?" he asked.

The fairy nodded. "You were at the keep."

"Yes, when it fell," he replied. "What are you doing here?"

Randiriel turned to face him, her skin papery and muted. "I'm holding on. It's harder without the Tear, but possible."

"I thought that fairies never held on."

Randiriel laughed. "That's what the girl said. But we're hardly fairies now, are we? We're something different, something new."

Geuel sat down on a bench along the wall. "How's that?"

"We were the city. We were the Tear. We were each other. Look at the city."

"It's fading," Geuel said.

Randiriel nodded. "But I'm not. The others aren't. The flowers broke. The city's fading. But I'm still here. There is no *we* anymore, just I and you and he and she."

"Is that why you're holding on?" Geuel asked.

"I'm holding on because I *want* to hold on."

"Why did you stay? Yesterday? You stayed when the others ran."

"Not all," Randiriel replied. "Ariel stayed. Ariel will always stay. She's not like the rest of us. She cries . . . I've seen her. Not with tears. We don't have tears. But in her eyes, she weeps. I wanted to weep."

"Most people hate to weep," Geuel said. "Isn't that what being a fairy is all about?"

"Perhaps," Randiriel replied, "but we're not fairies. Fairies are pure."

"You're not pure?" Geuel asked.

"I've felt the pain," Randiriel said. "I don't know about the others, but yesterday *I* felt life's pain. Fairies don't feel pain. Only Ariel."

"Out there," Geuel gestured to the horizon, "we all feel pain. We consider it the cost of beauty."

"And is it worth it?" Randiriel asked.

"Yes," Geuel said. "There's a flag out there somewhere, a Golden Iris sown in sky-blue silk. Men have bled for it, laughed under it, sang of it, and been buried with it wrapped around their shoulders. And every one of them would bleed again, just to see it wave where it has never waved before. There's nothing more beautiful."

"I will see this flag someday," Randiriel said.

Geuel smiled. "Tell me then if beauty is worth its cost."

Just then Veil came running in through the door. "Geuel," she said, "Hefthon's back. Mother says we need to eat now."

Geuel nodded. "All right, Veil. I'll be along." He turned back to Randiriel. "I hope you can hold on," he said.

As Geuel entered the opposing building, a bright, red-dressed figure caught his eye on the counter. Ariel smiled. "Enjoy your visit with Rand?" she asked.

Geuel clapped his brother on the back in greeting and nodded to Ariel. "Enlightening, at least. I thought fairies drew their power from the Tear."

"They do—in a way," Ariel replied. "The Tear is linked to Innocence. It is her cyntras that we use in wielding it. But our connection to the Tear has left us with some of our own cyntras. That is what we use now. My brothers and sisters, those remaining of the nine, can keep the city standing. But that is all. It will continue to fade."

"And the other fairies?" Geuel asked.

"Frightened, confused," Hefthon said, "they won't help with anything."

Ariel nodded. "The Tear connected our emotions as well as our power. They do not know how to feel alone. So, they are regressing past childhood, almost to an infant state."

"Not Randiriel," Geuel replied. "She seems as strong as you."

"Perhaps she is. She is no more a child now than I. She has discovered self and will only grow stronger in isolation."

"And why can't the others grow stronger?" Geuel asked. "What's so special about Randiriel?"

"We call this city The City of Youth," Ariel replied. "But a truer title might call it The City of Innocence. What we save here is not all of childhood. It is just that part which we call most beautiful: the wondering innocence and untainted curiosity that makes the poets write of childhood as if it were godhood. The fairies are not merely linked to Innocence. They are part of her, living manifestations of the Trait herself, governed by their own hearts and minds but saturated by Innocence. Without Innocence, the fairies have no identity."

"And Randiriel?" Geuel asked.

"I do not quite know," Ariel replied.

Tressa handed Geuel and Hefthon each a sandwich. "Well, let's hope that Reheuel finds the Tear then."

"For their sake," Geuel replied, tilting his head toward the city's center.

"For all our sakes," Ariel replied. "The goblins did not take the gem as a bauble. They will use it as a weapon."

Hefthon stiffened. "The Tear is linked to Innocence. Surely no goblin could wield her cyntras."

"The fairies access Innocence through the Tear," Ariel replied, "but there are other Passions and Traits who had their hand in its making. You know my story. When my father died, I shed my innocence through my tears. But I felt other things as well: anger and hatred and malice. All of those feelings are bound inside the Tear. And any one might be used by a goblin."

Hefthon paled. "There's only one reason that the goblins would want such a weapon now . . ."

"Gath Odrenoch," Geuel said. He glanced to the wall where his sword leaned. "I'm going after Father," he said. "If the Tear is that important, they won't leave it with a raiding party for long."

Hefthon moved into another room and returned with his longbow. He tossed it to Geuel. "You gave yours to Father," he said.

Geuel nodded. "Keep watch here, brother. When I return, be ready to leave. We ride for home."

Hefthon grasped his shoulder. "Be safe."

"Always." He turned to Tressa. "Sorry, Mother, but I must."

She nodded. "We'll be fine."

Geuel stepped out into the street and headed for the building where Iridius was stabled.

Tressa looked over at Ariel. "Why didn't you say anything before?" she asked.

"I did not want Reheuel to fear," Ariel replied. "He would have been reckless."

Veil hugged her mother's waist. "Where's Geuel going?" she asked.

"To fetch Father," Tressa whispered, still staring mistrustfully at Ariel.

* * *

The fire smoldered dully in the night, casting dark shadows on the still, silent goblins sitting around it. Their eyes were closed and their mouths set. A slab of horse meat roasted on a sickle over the fire, filling the air with the scent of burning flesh.

Four more goblins crept into the firelight, nickering and snuffling at the air. They pulled themselves along with the tips of their fingers and toes, scuttling on all fours in silence. The sitters said nothing, eyes closed.

One of the newcomers approached the edge of the firelight and shook one of the sitters by the shoulder. It slumped stiffly to the ground, uprooting the arrow that had held it in place. The goblin shrieked.

An arrow hissed in the night.

* * *

It was nearly twilight when Geuel reached the site of his father's skirmish. He had ridden far faster than Reheuel had dared, but still he lagged many hours behind. He found the horse first, dragged behind a stand of poplar and mutilated, a massive chunk of meat carved from its thigh. Next, he found the campsite.

There were eight bodies in all, four sitting stiffly around the campfire, backs propped on logs and arrows pinning their thighs to the ground. Four more lay scattered with their backs to the fire. Arrows protruded from every body.

The air smelled of burning meat, and the coals were still warm.

Geuel traced the arrows in the goblins' backs to the east of the fire. In a stand of young pine, he found the archer's hiding spot. Downwind, obscured by the boughs of the pine. Just the kind of place Reheuel would hide. Heavy boot marks, scuffed with shifts of weight, rested in the earth beside one of the trees. He had waited for a long time. Large red slicks covered the trunk where he had leaned. Geuel grit his teeth. He was wounded, and more than once.

Further into the pines, Geuel found some snapped boughs, several spotted with blood. His father was moving erratically. What footsteps Geuel could find were unsteady and inconsistent. He spurred his horse forward. The tracks led to the east. He had to be heading for the Faeja.

Chapter 5

In Elicathaliss, Ariel floated in the center of an open room facing Randiriel. "You can't keep doing this, Rand. You're wearing yourself out." She touched Randiriel's forehead. "You've gone cold."

"I can't let go. No one else is building now. I used to feel them, all around, two thousand souls dreaming, yearning, and building. And now—nothing. Have you seen them Ariel? The flowers in the walkways, the moving mazes in the sky, the towers that surrounded the city, the clockwork, diamond monsters that swam in the Faeja . . . they're all gone."

"Yes, I've seen. But they can be built again. You don't have the strength to hold these things alone." Ariel gestured to the flowers and the sculptures in the room, fewer now than when Geuel had visited. Little piles of colored dust marked the places where those missing had finally faded.

"What is the point of us if we end now, if nothing remains?" Randiriel asked. "A thousand years we've lived in this city. Will one day end it all? We've wasted so much time, built so little. Something needs to last."

Ariel lifted a crystal flower. In her hand it was the size of a walking stick. It blossomed and glowed as she clutched it, its clear petals flushing with color. "We will last, Rand. And we will build again. But you can't keep this up. You'll die."

Randiriel stared at the flower in Ariel's hand. She reached out and grasped it. "Just this one," she whispered. As she lifted it, the other flowers and sculptures in the room disintegrated, showering the floor in new piles of dust

Ariel smiled. "Focus on that one, Rand. And try to rest. Your light is dim."

Randiriel sank slowly to the floor and settled onto one of the tiles, letting the flower down beside her. She curled into a ball and stared at the flower's ruby petals, inhaling the scent of fire and rose. Her voice fell to a murmur as her body resigned itself to exhaustion. "What will happen, Ariel? If he finds the tear?"

Ariel landed beside her and laid her hand upon Randiriel's shoulder. "Our sisters and brothers will be reunited," she said. "There will be great joy and building. The memories of yesterday will fade beneath brighter emotions."

"And me?" Randiriel asked. "What will happen to me?"

"I—do not know," Ariel said. "You are different from the others. They will forget beneath each other's emotions."

"I don't want to forget," Randiriel said softly. "For one day I fought beside the council. I don't want to forget that." Randiriel's eyes flickered sleepily, and her voice droned.

"I don't believe you will," Ariel replied, a slight catch in her voice.

"Are you weeping, Ariel?"

"Yes, Sister," Ariel replied.

"I want to weep someday. I wept before, you know, when I was a girl. I had forgotten, but I remember so much now."

"Perhaps you will again."

"I remember my mother, her face."

Ariel stroked her head. "You cannot, Rand. You were too young."

Randiriel shook her head. "No, I see her now. She was beautiful. I was so very sad when she died. I guess I forgot. Maybe that's why I was able to become a fairy, because I forgot."

"Perhaps."

Randiriel's eyes closed. "I don't want to forget anymore," she whispered as the last of her consciousness faded.

Ariel patted her sleeping form. "You will not have to. Only fairies forget." She stood and fluttered through the door. Her flight dragged, and her arms hung listlessly at her sides. Her eyes pooled with dry sorrow. If fairies could weep.

* * *

That evening, Veil sat in the keep. Behind her, several fairies fluttered about, braiding her hair. They giggled as they worked, glimmering brightly. "And then in the Year of Pilgrimage, we all gather in groups," said one.

"Nine groups," interrupted another.

"One for each of the Council," the first finished.

"And we leave on the stroke of midnight on the first day of the harvest."

"And fly over all of Rehavan."

"Well, not all."

"Most, definitely. And we see all the races and people."

"We get to sleep in the forests, curled in leaves or hidden in the notches of the diamond trees."

"That's my favorite part, to sleep in the diamond trees. They sing when the wind blows through. Their clear wood fills with light like crystal in the morning, and we wake up inside of rainbows."

"I like to see the ocean."

"Sometimes we build ships of light and set them sailing for the horizon."

Veil laughed. "So, you all love to travel?"

As she spoke, others of the fairies came and gathered around her, drifting from the alcoves and hidden recesses of the great hall, from their hideaways in the ceiling and their miniature houses in the chandeliers. One of the fairies on the steps spoke up. "Travel is our favorite time."

"Not mine," said another.

The rest grew silent, as if unsure how to handle dissent.

"Have you ever seen the dwarves?" Veil asked. "Father says that they've hidden away since the Iris was sewn."

"Oh, yes," I've seen the dwarves, many times, said one of the fairies. "They live in the Khaien mountains. We visit their city of Unkhai."

"What are they like?" Veil asked.

"Ugly," said a younger fairy.

The others laughed. "They're slow," said one, "and proud. And they have big beards."

"Ugly," repeated the younger fairy, delighted with the success of its joke.

Tressa stood in the archway with Ariel floating beside her. "She has a healing heart," Tressa said. "Even on the farm she's always caring for the sickly animals."

Ariel smiled. "It's good to see them laughing. Veil is the best thing they could have right now. A true child to remind them what they are."

Randiriel flitted up beside Ariel from a nearby ledge. "Do *you* know what they are, though?"

Ariel nodded. "My children," she said, "my innocent children."

                                    * * *

Night fell as Geuel reached the river. It lay, calm and wide in the glow of the waxing moon. He walked his horse south along the bank for a few miles, occasionally spotting footprints in the mud. He found a knot of discarded makeshift bandages, stained deep red despite their rinsing. Reheuel couldn't have made it far.

An hour later, he saw a prone form in the grass near the riverbank, barely noticeable in the half-light. He leapt from his horse. "Father?" he asked. He approached and placed his fingers on Reheuel's neck. A faint pulse trickled beneath his fingertips. "What have you done to yourself?" he asked, peeling back his father's shirt to see the wound. "Brash old man."

He dug his hands down under Reheuel's shoulders and knees. "Sorry," he said and lifted.

Reheuel groaned in his sleep and muttered. Geuel lay his body across the front of his saddle and tied his arms and legs into place with bowstrings.

He then climbed up behind and spurred his horse. "Gently, Iridius," he whispered.

The trees flashed by in the night. Rocks occasionally clacked beneath the horse's hooves in the fields, and logs thudded on its calves in the forests. Every minute, Geuel waited for Iridius to lurch and whinny, to collapse with a broken leg from some root or tree trunk. But still he nudged him faster.

Reheuel's head lolled on the saddle, occasionally bouncing against the hard leather when the horse landed a harder step. Geuel laid a hand on his head. "Hold on, Father," he said. "Just to the city. Be strong, old man."

Twice during the ride, Geuel heard the shrieks of goblins in the woods, both times distant and unintelligible. He shuddered, nonetheless. They were out in force. He prayed silently to Curiosity to spare Gath Odrenoch. To spare his people.

He wondered often what ghastly power the Tear would obtain, wielded with the cyntras of Anger or Malice. Was it already being used? Did Gath Odrenoch burn? He pictured the log walls and rickety spires of the city, the stone barracks behind the governor's double-story mansion, the well dug by his uncle. He spurred his horse harder. The city would not burn. Not without him inside.

* * *

"And off that way, far beyond the farthest Iris, lie the Western mountains. They catch the rain clouds that would travel west and keep Rehavan lush in the summer,"

Hefthon said, pointing to the west from the top of the fairy keep.

"And what's past the mountains?" Veil asked.

"Not much," Hefthon replied. The desert, mostly. There are people there, though, humans like us. Their nearest city is Calymore in the foothills of the mountains."

"Anything else?" Veil asked, knowing the answer but wishing to hear it again.

"Well, there are the sand dragons in the loneliest areas, giant creatures that burrow into the earth and ambush their prey. Then there are the sand people. Some say they were men once, cursed by Ingway to live forever between dust and flesh."

Veil grinned. "I want to travel there some day."

Hefthon ruffled her hair. "Of all the places? Not to Esrathel or Elisidor? Why the desert?"

"There must be people who need help."

"I guess there probably are," Hefthon replied. He turned back to the east. The sun was just clearing the edge of the horizon, striking the pale sides of Elicathaliss and tinting them a rosy pink. "But there is plenty to do here as well."

Veil pointed to the north. "Is that something moving?"

Hefthon followed her finger carefully and saw a dark form rapidly crossing the plains by the river. "Yes," he said. "Looks like a rider." He headed for the stairs. "Perhaps it's Geuel or Father. Come on,"

As he stepped out of the building on the first floor, he felt the earth give way beneath his right foot. He collapsed downward, his leg sinking through the shattered crystal pavement. Below, he heard slabs of crystal splash into the flow of the Faeja. With the gap in the road, the river could be heard plainly below.

Veil screamed.

Hefthon kept perfectly still, one leg spread out over the ground and the other hanging down in a jagged hole. Tressa reached out her hand. "Take my hand, quickly."

He grasped her wrist, and she pulled him upright, his leg sliding out of the hole.

Tressa knelt to examine the place where he had fallen. The road was only about six inches thick. About thirty feet below, she could see the Faeja. "There are cracks," she said, "spreading out from the hole. We'll need to use the other entrance when we come back here."

Hefthon nodded. "The city's getting weaker by the hour."

Together they made their way along the street toward the north gate. It lay about a half-mile to the north. When they reached it and climbed the wall, they could see the figure clearly in the distance. A single rider with a load. Hefthon paled. "Father." He turned to Veil. "Go tell Ariel to meet us. We'll need her."

Tressa placed her hand on her son's shoulder. "Be calm," she whispered. "We don't know yet." Her hand trembled where it rested.

Hefthon grasped her hand in his own and squeezed it. "He'll be all right," he said. Turning to the gate, he found the wheel for the portcullis and began turning it. The silver bars of the gate trembled as they rose, and several broke off as the spikes left their moorings.

"So much for locking the gates," Hefthon said.

Tressa looked around nervously. "The city is rotting. What will happen when the towers weaken?"

Several minutes later, the rider came close enough for Hefthon to recognize him. "It's Geuel," he said. "Looks like he has someone on the saddle." He looked back into the city. "Where's Veil?"

When Geuel reached the gate, he stopped his horse and slid out of the saddle. As soon as his feet touched the ground, he collapsed. "Get him—get him to the keep," he said.

The horse stood heaving in the gateway, her breaths deep and hard. Geuel patted her leg. "Good girl," he said.

Tressa ran to her husband. "Reh?" she asked, "Reh?" She leapt up into the saddle behind him and snapped the reins. "Find Ariel," she called over her shoulder.

Hefthon extended a hand to Geuel. "Come on, brother."

Geuel let himself be dragged upright and wiped a slick of sweat from his forehead. "Long ride," he said.

"Tell me about it later," Hefthon replied. "Did he find the tear?"

Geuel shook his head. "Wasn't on him."

"City's going to pieces," Hefthon said, pointing to a tower on the corner. "Been watching that one, it'll fall at any moment. Already twisted part way."

Geuel nodded as they walked down the road. "Yeah," he said as his breath returned, "saw some gaps in the wall on the way up. Stones jumbled on the banks."

"How's Father?"

Geuel shook his head. "Doesn't look good. He's lost a lot of blood. Brash old man."

"Don't do that," Hefthon said.

"Do what?"

"He might die,"

"Yeah, well, he'd still be safe if he hadn't charged off alone. He's not thirty anymore—or forty for that matter."

"He's a brave man."

"He's a great man," Geuel replied, "but that doesn't make him any younger."

Hefthon nodded ahead. "Iridius is by the door. You should put her with the other horses. Oh, and watch your footing." Hefthon pointed to the hole in the street.

"Good to know," Geuel replied.

Hefthon heard sobbing as he entered the keep. Reheuel lay near the middle of the main hall with his head resting on a saddle. The bow and saddlebags lay in a jumble nearby. Veil knelt beside him, shuddering violently, her face burrowed into Tressa's shoulder. Tressa sat still and dry-eyed, Reheuel's right hand clasped in hers over his chest. With her other hand, she stroked her daughter's hair.

Ariel hovered with her council a short ways off. They were whispering, but their voices echoed in the empty chamber.

Hefthon approached. "Can you do anything?" he asked.

Ariel turned away from the others to face him. "We could—with the Tear. Healing is natural to us. But, as is, I do not know. It has taken all we have to hold the city together."

Hefthon pointed to his father. "He did this for you."

"I don't know what will happen to the city."

"Does it matter?" Hefthon asked. "The Tear's gone. How long can you hold out? A day, two?"

Randiriel approached from near the stairs. "I can help," she said.

Ariel nodded. "Help them hold the keep. The rest of the city can fade."

She pointed to two of the council. "Celine, Brylle, help me."

Hefthon glanced around. "What do you mean, just the keep?" he asked.

Ariel waved her arm toward the walls outside. "All of that shall fade. We will hold this building intact—if we can."

"Wait, I have to get Geuel," Hefthon said, "and the horses." He ran outside. "Geuel!" he called. "Bring the horses. Geuel!"

A loud groan followed by staccato splinters and cracks sounded from across the road. Horses whinnied in fear.

Hefthon ran for the stables. "Geuel?" he shouted. As he approached the door, he felt the ground shift beneath his feet, its brittle surface cracking under unnatural contortions. He blotted out the sounds and ran through the archway, only to stagger to a halt at the edge of a great chasm. Five feet of empty space spread from one wall to the other—a solid chunk of the city's floor just gone.

Geuel stood on the far side of the gap, his back pressed to the wall. The horses were gone.

"Hefthon eyed the gap. "Can you jump it?" he asked.

Geuel nodded doubtfully.

"The fairies are releasing the city," he said. "You have to come now." He spread his arms. "Aim for me. I'm far enough back"

Geuel stepped away from the wall and bent his knees. "Just like hopping the crik back home," he said.

Hefthon glanced quickly at the massive river thirty feet below. "Yeah—just like that."

Geuel ran and leapt. His shoulder struck Hefthon in the chest, and they both stumbled backward into the wall. It shattered and crumbled behind them, and they rolled out into the street, covered in silver dust.

Hefthon wiped a spot of blood from his cheek. "Not so bad," he said, slapping his brother on the back. "You okay?"

Geuel trembled slightly as he stood up. "Let's get inside."

Hefthon kicked the damaged wall behind them and watched it crumble. "Right behind you," he said.

They entered the keep together and found the main hall crowded and filled with chatter. More than sixteen hundred fairies clustered from floor to ceiling through the whole four floors. Flitting to and fro and babbling wildly. Randiriel and the council knelt in a ring holding hands near the stairs. In the center of the room, Ariel and her two sisters hovered over Reheuel.

Ariel looked over to the brothers. "Lock the doors," she said. "No matter what happens, do not interrupt us." She turned around. "Let us start."

Seconds later, a great roar drowned out all noise. The keep trembled and shook, and the fairies screamed, flashing back and forth and batting at the walls, trying to find a way out through the locked windows. Hefthon stumbled and braced himself against the wall. Tressa clutched Veil against the stairs. Geuel staggered unsteadily.

The ground shuddered again, and a massive crack echoed through the room from outside. "Half the city must have fallen away," Geuel cried out.

"No splash," Hefthon replied. "It's just the towers falling into the city."

Just then a mighty groan drowned out their voices. Veil clutched her hands over her ears and cried out. The keep keeled over to one side, hurling Geuel against the wall and throwing Hefthon to the ground. A deep roar sounded from the water below as the river struggled over a section of the city. Splashed water, running down the sides of the keep, trickled through the crack of the door.

In the center of the room, Ariel hovered over Reheuel, gleaming brighter than Geuel had ever seen her, her scarlet dress blazing like a ruby in the sunlight. Her hands were stretched out to Reheuel's face, and they trembled as if in exhaustion. Her eyes were closed.

"Hold on," Geuel said, "hold on."

The keep shuddered again and slid downward. Geuel felt his stomach shift suddenly, and for one single moment he felt weightless. Then he was falling. Falling with the keep toward the water. Veil screamed.

A roaring crash sounded from below, and Geuel and the others slammed bodily to the floor as the keep struck the

Faeja's surface. Water ran in through the cracks of the doors
and window shades. Fairies flew upward, shrieking madly
and clustering near the roof in a rustling, glowing mass.
Geuel dragged himself to his feet and staggered toward his
mother. "The stairs!" he called. "Up the stairs."

Tressa dragged Veil onto the steps and began climbing,
Hefthon placing his hand on her back.

Geuel went back toward Reheuel and sank beside him.
He was still unconscious, but the water ran about his body,
slowly building upward—already nearly two inches deep.
Tickling his ears. Ariel and the other two fairies still
hovered above him in silence, as if oblivious to the water, to
the fact that their tower stood on the floor of the Faeja.

Geuel could hear the current outside, striking and
churning around the silver walls. The keep had settled,
sitting vertically in the center of the Faeja. He looked to the
stairs. The council were still there, hands held tightly,
bodies taut with exertion. As he watched, one body went
limp. Its light flickered, and it fell, splashing in the three-
inch water on the floor. Geuel ran over and scooped it up,
pulling it from under the water and setting it on the steps.
Its eyes were glazed, but it seemed alive. Geuel looked to
the other council members. "Come on," he said, "you have
to do something."

The water still rose around Reheuel, nearly past his ears
now. Soon it would cover his mouth. Just as it broke over
the corners of his lips, a bright flash of light bloomed in the
center of the council ring. Randiriel's body blazed as
brightly as Ariel's, her skin burning like the sun, her green
dress a fluorescent glow. The rest of the council paled
beside her. Her body slowly rose, eyes still closed and
muscles stiff. She slipped from the grasp of her fellows and
rose higher, dragging her tense arms up from her sides as if
pulling some great weight. The keep lifted.

On the stairs, Hefthon gasped. "Geuel, the door!" he called.

Randiriel continued to ascend, burning ever brighter as she lifted, soon eclipsing even Ariel. The keep trembled but rose also, the sound of rushing water engulfing it on every side.

Geuel stood by the door and lifted his sword. "Are we clear?" he called. Hefthon watched the trickles of water at the window slowly disappearing. "Wait, wait," he called.

"Are we clear?"

"Now!" Hefthon called.

Geuel slid his sword into the tight seam between the doors and pried one of them back into its slot in the wall. Water rushed out through the opening, draining over the edge of the floor. Geuel braced himself in the door frame and stared outside, water rushing about his ankles and splashing in the river below.

The keep rested barely a foot over the surface of the Faeja. Towers and walls and roads projected haphazardly all about, cluttering the water and jutting upward like the debris of a silver avalanche. The keep kept on rising, and slowly the Faeja fell away, swollen out over its banks around the ruins of Elicathaliss.

"Randiriel, turn!" he cried. "Get us onto the plain."

Slowly, the keep shifted direction and drifted toward the shore. The silver stones groaned and rumbled as they moved.

A gasp came from the center of the room, followed by a sputtering choke. Reheuel sat up and coughed, emptying his lungs of water. Tressa ran to him.

Hefthon stayed on the stairs staring at Randiriel. She was barely visible anymore as a form. Just a sphere of blinding light. "Help her," he called. "Ariel!"

Ariel ascended beside Randiriel and clasped her hand. The light distributed between them, and after a few seconds the tower sank to the earth on the Faeja's shores.

Ariel smiled. "Well done, Rand," she said softly.

Randiriel drifted unsteadily to the floor and leant against the leg of a bench. Her skin was pale and sickly, her light dimming to a dull, ember-like glow.

Chapter 6

Reheuel stood slowly in the middle of the keep, staring in confusion at the water and the open door. Tressa wrapped her arms tightly around her husband and kissed his cheek. "Reh," she said, gasping, "I thought I'd lost you."

He stroked her hair softly, feeling her body warming him through his soaked clothing. "I'm not going anywhere," he whispered. "Not for a while."

Ariel drifted closer to the couple. "Did you find the Tear?" she asked.

Reheuel shook his head as he slowly pulled away from his wife, kissing her lips as they parted. "I couldn't catch up with all of them. They took it to the mountain."

"I fear what will happen if they use it," Ariel said. "The Tear had the power to create a race. Faeja knows how much it might destroy."

"I'm sorry, Ariel. I tried," Reheuel replied. He paused then. "But how did I get here? I was—by the river."

Geuel rose from the steps. "I tracked you and brought you back. Ariel healed you. But that's not important. We have other concerns. What if the goblins use the Tear against Gath Odrenoch?"

"They won't," Reheuel replied. "Geuel, Hefthon, I want you to take your mother and Veil back to Gath Odrenoch. Warn them what might be coming."

Tressa grabbed his wrist. "No! Come home. You can't do this alone. Gather your men first. Kezeik, Deni. You've done enough."

Reheuel pulled her close and gripped her tightly, feeling her body shudder inside his arms. "I'm the Captain of the Guards, Love. I'm responsible for our city."

Tressa ran her fingers through the gash in his cotton shirt. "You've already bled for them today."

Reheuel closed his eyes to stop his tears. "Do you love me?" he whispered.

"Always,"

"The man you love would go," he said.

They ended their embrace, and Reheuel turned to his sons. "Be strong, boys. Protect your mother and your sister."

Geuel shook his head. "You're not a young man anymore." Hefthon struck his brother's shoulder, but Geuel continued. "You can't just run off and save the day—break down the gates with a battering ram and pull the arrows from your chest to reuse later."

Reheuel placed his hand on his son's shoulder. "I have to try."

"You'll die," Geuel said. "Forgive my disrespect. But you *will* die."

Reheuel nodded. "Then forgive me when I do."

Veil ran up to him and threw her arms around his waist. "Goodbye, Father," she said, sobbing but struggling to sound strong.

Reheuel knelt down. "Goodbye, my Passion. Take care of your brothers."

Ariel flew to his shoulder. "I'll come with you," she said. "The Tear is part of me. I can help you find it."

She turned to address the council, but they were all still weak, lying scattered on the stones, some unconscious. Randiriel alone still stood, leaning against the edge of the stairs.

"Take care of our people, Rand," Ariel said. "Be strong for them."

Geuel and Hefthon began packing up what items they had not lost with the horses, Geuel handing back Hefthon's unused bow, and Ariel landed once more on the stairs. Tressa approached her and whispered, "Don't let him die for your troubles."

Within twenty minutes, Reheuel's family were all hiking away from the keep. Reheuel and Ariel approached the edge of the Faeja, stopping at a place just above the wreckage of the city. Ariel drew a silver flute-like instrument from her belt and began to play, the sounds carrying far over the water to the north. The music chortled slightly, like the sound of a brook or a stream; and the rhythms surged and receded like a surf, perfectly constant.

After a few minutes, the water stirred, and faces appeared in the currents. They were like disturbances carved in the ripples, there one moment and gone the next, their hair flowing, long and wild in the eddies that surrounded their faces. Reheuel could hardly tell if they were solid or liquid. They seemed to flow and move with the water, to distort in the current. But, at the same time, they rested almost beneath the surface, like a swimmer staring from just beneath the water.

Ariel put away her flute and spoke to them in a language full of babble and the gush of water, rushing with a kind of raw beauty, wholly foreign to the tinkling silver of the fairy voice.

"What are we doing?" Reheuel asked, anxious to leave.

"Transportation," Ariel replied. "The river sprites will help us reach the mountain."

A few minutes later the river swelled slightly, waves sloshing over the bank. The eddies quickened around the boulders that broke the surface, and waves appeared where before the water had been smooth. The river rose continually, running faster and faster as it struggled through the wreckage that clotted it. After several minutes, a small rowboat came into sight upstream, borne rapidly in a solitary surge. It looked strangely out of place, the rough-hewn timber boat, caught in the supernatural rapids around it, pounding water filled with the laughing faces of the sprites.

The boat nosed gently into the bank beside Reheuel, and the water slowed to its normal calm. Ariel flew out over the river and thanked the sprites in their language, holding out her hand as if in blessing.

Reheuel stepped carefully into the boat. "No oars," he said, glancing at the floor of the craft.

"We won't need them," Ariel replied as she landed on the boat's prow. She pointed upstream and spoke a command to the sprites.

The boat turned in the water and swung out from the shore, lifting slightly in the prow as a new current took hold of it. It moved steadily upstream, faster even than Reheuel could have rowed it. On either side the water still ran past downstream, but where the boat moved, a single reverse current grew below. Glancing over the edge of the boat, Reheuel saw waves lift and slide forward against the boat's bottom. Occasionally, fingers and hands of water formed in the waves, dragging and pushing at the boat and then dissipating back into the current.

Ariel lay down in the prow and wrapped her wings around her arms and chest, sheltering herself from the breeze of their movement. "What do you plan to do, once we reach the mountain?" she asked.

Reheuel shrugged. "I don't really know. We'll have to be quiet. There could be hundreds of them, perhaps more by now. It's been so long."

Ariel nodded. "I can lead you to the caves, but you will have to find our way in."

"You know I've been to the caves before?"

Ariel nodded.

"So why did you come?"

"Because you have no duty toward my people . . . I do."

The boat continued for hours, and after a while, Reheuel lay down to sleep. His side ached dully, and he could feel the scar on his back rubbing against the wood hull of the boat. The wound was healed, as was that on his leg, but even Ariel's magic could not replace the blood he had lost. Exhaustion still plagued him. The little boat continued for hours as he slept, racing with unnatural speed.

* * *

"Seven days' hike . . ." Geuel muttered as he crested a hill, shoving off of his ash walking stick. "What I wouldn't give to have kept the horses."

Hefthon nodded. "It'd be easy enough with just the two of us. But I don't know if Veil can do it even in seven. I think she'll take nine. Not to mention finding food."

"I could do it in four alone," Geuel said. "I feel so helpless."

Hefthon glanced back at his mother and sister as they climbed the hill behind him. "Go," he said. "You're faster than I am anyway."

Geuel shifted uncomfortably, anxious to leave but unsure of his duty. "I feel like I'm deserting you."

Hefthon shook his head. "The goblins are long gone. There's little danger left out here. How much food do you have?"

"About two days' worth."

Hefthon unslung his pack. "Take mine. We can stop and hunt along the way. You need to warn the others, to get everyone inside the walls."

Geuel took the pack uncertainly. "You sure?"

"We both know you have to. Don't force guilt."

Geuel nodded and set off at a light lope down the far side of the hill. Hefthon turned and helped Veil over the hill's crest. "Easy there," he said.

Tressa reached the top of the hill a moment later. "Is Geuel gone?" she asked.

Hefthon nodded.

"Good," she said.

* * *

Reheuel awoke to the dull shadows of a forest, heavy across the water in the dim light of early morning. High above and seemingly just miles distant, the first mountain of the Gath chain rose bright and welcoming, strangely beautiful given the darkness that dwelt just beyond. Off beyond its edges, Reheuel could see farther mountains of the range, Tubath and Henerrin just visible in the distance. He knew that somewhere between those two spires Gath Odrenoch lay nestled. "Did we travel all night?" he asked.

Ariel, still wrapped in her wings in the prow, nodded. "The Sprites never tire in the water. We should reach the mountain this afternoon."

"We should have brought the others. Saved them time."

"We are in the foothills now," Ariel replied. "They would waste days finding usable routes."

Reheuel opened his pack and drew out some dried meat. "Feels strange to be moving so fast without effort. Makes me restless."

Ariel nodded. "I flew part of the night."

"So, what happens if we don't find the Tear? To the fairies I mean?" Reheuel asked as he ate.

"They will age," Ariel replied, "shed their innocence and find adulthood. Most will die. Starvation, cold, violence. Without the Tear, they may even get sick. The fairies have been sheltered since childhood, living without struggle or pain, all linked by the Tear. Most were weak even before they became fairies."

"And if we find the Tear? What then?"

"I would hope that things can be restored," Ariel said. "But the trauma, the pain, the development—could all that really be forgotten? To stay young, the fairies require innocence, ignorance. For many it will be too late."

"Like Randiriel, the one who fought?" Reheuel asked.

"Rand's—different," Ariel replied, struggling with the words. "Randiriel was—a mistake. I took her after her innocence had ended. Randiriel was lost as a fairy before she became one. There is no going back for her."

"And what will happen to those like her, the ones who can't go back?"

Ariel shrugged. "Some will join the council. Others . . . like Randiriel . . . will leave. Randiriel is strong. Far stronger than her brothers and sisters. She will survive."

"So, you'll banish her?" Reheuel asked.

"Without innocence, no being could happily endure our ignorance," Ariel replied. "She will need to explore, to see the world, to find the wonder and the ugliness of it. There will be no place for her in the City of Youth."

"Why do you stay then? You're no longer innocent," Reheuel asked.

"I have purpose there. I protect my people, just as you protect yours. As long as my actions fall in suit with Innocence, my tie to her remains. Besides, I've seen enough of the world's ugliness. Elicathaliss offers no ignorance for me."

Reheuel laughed. "I used to think that the Fairy City was so perfect, so eternal."

"So did I," Ariel replied sadly.

"It was pure, unblemished, a lingering taste of childhood," Reheuel said. "But childhood never lasts alone, does it? It's too frail. You're the one who's kept it alive, a bitter adult sheltering artificial youth."

"Adults always shelter youth. Without you to provide, would your children ever have had a time of innocence? You took the pain that life threw at them—the struggles, the responsibilities. You bore the weight of their living. My protection does not falsify my city's youth. It completes it."

Reheuel grew silent and turned his eyes back to the riverbanks. The Faeja was smaller near the mountain, narrower and slightly faster than the tributary-swollen, lazy river that flowed beneath Elicathaliss. The banks were in clear sight on either side, covered in thick sedge broken occasionally by little stands of purple loosestrife. Occasionally, he could see the blue and yellow of irises peeking out from behind the bulrushes. He fingered the iris stitched into his tunic and felt a rush of bile in his throat, burning and putrid. His city balanced on the edge of destruction, and the Iris wanted conscripts for her conquests.

The nation was rotting.

* * *

Geuel awoke with a start, scrabbling to his feet and struggling with the folds of his cloak. He slapped wildly at his face, at the soft, tingling pricks that stretched across it. A large wolf spider flew to the ground and scurried away into the loam. Geuel's racing heart stilled. Just a spider, he told himself. Just a spider. He shook himself to clear his head and slapped at his breeches, shifting the dewy cotton where it clung to his legs. Dawn had passed, and the sun hung just above the eastern horizon, pink-hued behind a haze of thin cloud.

He lifted his packs from the ground and cinched them tightly to his back. Three more days, four at the most. He had traveled longer than usual, finally collapsing at the feet of a large diamond tree near midnight. He started walking and winced as his joints groaned beneath him. He was a strong hiker, well accustomed to long days and nights spent sprawled over the roots and pebbles of the forest. But he knew that even his body would struggle to maintain the twenty-mile days ahead of him.

Hour after hour throughout that second day, he dragged himself onward, sometimes half-sprinting down inclines, other times stumbling breathlessly to crest a hill. Rarely pausing, knowing that to stop would invite the full force of his fatigue to catch up with him. Knowing that if he once laid down, he would not rise for hours.

His throat was perpetually dry, and his body burned beneath a layer of sweat. But he dared not drink too often for fear of slowing his pace. He sucked on a flat pebble to moisten his mouth and sought the shadiest routes.

The day dragged by slowly, morning melting beneath noon's oppressive heat, the heat seeming to linger eternally, reticent to surrender to evening's chill. When evening finally came, the sweat that saturated Geuel's clothing cooled miserably and clung, sticky but cold, to his skin. The breeze that hours earlier would have been a welcome relief merely served to chill him further. He yearned to stop and start a fire, to sleep with his back to the embers until the last ray of heat had leaked from the ashes and died in the next day's morning. Instead, around ten thirty that night, he collapsed against the trunk of a great cedar tree, wrapped his cloak around his body, and struggled to forget the cold, to sleep through the misery of the night.

Despite his exhaustion, it took him over an hour to finally fall asleep. The cold seeped through the mesh of his cloak and infiltrated the lining of his jacket, caressing his skin with the freezing fingertips of night. No matter how he tucked the edges of his cloak behind him, sealing each gap, the cold still found a way in, still crept through some crevice between flesh and cloth. Occasionally he heard movements in the brush and trees, the pattering of little feet in the loam and the snuffling of moist snouts. Each time that he heard movement, he imagined goblins, spindled across the branches of nearby trees, waiting for him to sleep, waiting for him to become vulnerable. Eventually, he drew his sword and clutched it beside him, finding comfort in its solidity, in the visible gleam of its blade.

Smoke rose from the towers of Gath Odrenoch. Flaming meteors shaped like skulls exploded in the earth of the town square. The barracks was a smoking crater, surrounded by glowing splinters of beams and melted glass. Kezeik lay in the earth outside, his body charred and smoking, his hound nuzzling at his side.

Geuel watched in horror as the blacksmith's twelve-year-old son, Akazi, stood alone in the gate of the city, his father's sword drawn and a dozen goblins licking their blades in front of him. The blacksmith's body lay slumped against the wheel of the portcullis where he had tried to close the gate. His wife screamed from the steps of their home. Above the gate the Golden Iris still waved proudly, her blue folds rippling in the smoky breeze, her threading torn by passing arrows.

Geuel tried to run forward, but a sharp pain in his arm stopped him. He slumped back and tried to rise again. Again, the pain stopped him. Just then Master Deni ran to Akazi's side and waved him backward, yelled for him to take his mother away. The goblins surged forward, and Deni waited, a light smile on his thin lips, his old eyes more full of life than Geuel had ever seen them.

A goblin fell. Geuel tried to run forward to help, and again his arm stung sharply. He felt blood running warmly down his forearm and glanced at it. He was trapped, pinned down by his own sword. It was caught in an overturned carriage beside where he lay. Another goblin fell. A third. Geuel tore his sword from the carriage and leapt to his feet, a scream of rage choking into horror as he watched Deni's body strike the earth.

He hadn't reached them. He was too late.

Geuel awoke with a start. Dawn was long past, and the sun hung high in the east. The light was the bright yellow of a clear mid-morning. Blood trickled down his right arm from a shallow gash. His sword lay in the grass beside where he had slept. His mouth was dry, and he drank from his canteen. The cold water chased away the images of the night, letting him forget all save one. He still remembered clearly the Golden Iris waving in the smoke of the city, the one glimpse of beauty left in a scene of horror.

After eating, he left his sword where it lay, glad to be rid of the weight, and took off at a light trot, his body energized with new-found purpose.

* * *

On top of a chandelier in the fairy keep, the council sat at a tiny round table, hands folded and faces grave. "How much food is there?" Celine, one of the fairies who had healed Reheuel, asked.

Randiriel shook her head. "Enough for lunch, maybe. We still have eighteen hundred mouths to feed. Some of them should be foraging."

Several of the council members laughed.

"They can't forage. They can barely speak," said one.

"They haven't needed to," Randiriel replied. "We've coddled them, haven't let them *do* anything. They need drive. They're not linked anymore. They're individuals."

Another fairy shook his head. His body looked youthful, as all fairy bodies do. But his voice wavered with age. "Ariel would not wish it. The less they exert themselves, the easier it will be for them to forget."

"Well, maybe they won't forget. Maybe they can't," Randiriel replied. "Who are we to hold them back from growing stronger? Anyway, do we have another option? They have to eat, and we can't all leave here. The keep would collapse behind us."

The council member Brylle rose. "Very well, we shall gather them and give them their instructions. I only hope they can still function."

It took a few hours of coaxing and explaining, but gradually the council gathered the fairies into groups of a hundred or so each and instructed them on gathering food. The instructions were nothing new. The fairies had all spent countless hours scouring for strawberries beneath the meadow grass, milking the clover blossoms, and stealing honey from the beehives in the forest. But most of the fairies hardly seemed able to comprehend the instructions. They were fractured and confused, many still in shock after being separated from their fellows.

Randiriel stood in front of a hundred fairies. In her had she clutched her crystal rose, the sole remaining token of her creations. She looked into the eyes of several of the fairies, trying to gauge their emotions. "Brothers and sisters," she said softly, "I know you're frightened. I know you feel alone. But tonight, you must forget your fear. You must rise above it." She levitated the flower gently before them. Several gasped, and hands reached out to brush it, to assure themselves of its existence.

Randiriel smiled. "I am alone now, just like each of you. *I* and *you* —these words meant little to us before. But now you must own them. You must hold to them as you once held to *us*. Each of you is strong. Each of you is a being. You may not be linked by a Tear, but you are still fairy." She pulled the rose back into her hands. "And if I can still do this, then I know that each of you can do it as well."

She paused and waited for a response. Most of the fairies simply stared blankly. Some whispered and rustled with the first stirrings of thought. Thirteen stood and nodded in understanding. "What should we do?" one asked.

Randiriel beckoned them closer, separating them from the others. She pointed to the door. "I need you to go out there and gather in food for the others: raspberries, strawberries, honey if you can find it. There are probably still may berries on the Blue Hills. Gather what you can find."

They nodded and turned to the door. Many seemed relieved, as if they had longed for some form of action, some objective to replace their former unity. The rest of the fairies still huddled where Randiriel had first addressed them, shifting and whispering uncomfortably. Randiriel smiled at them. "You may all return to your places," she said.

Around the keep, in twos and tens and sevens and twelves, groups of fairies headed for the doors, the strong separating from the weak, the protectors from the innocent.

Chapter 7

Reheuel stepped slowly from the boat. His stomach churned, and he nearly slipped back into the water as he struggled up the muddy bank. He felt like vomiting but refrained, clinging to what slight bodily control he retained. The world swam before his eyes, caught up in the rhythm of motion that had blurred his vision for nearly two days.

Ariel flew out over the water and gave her thanks to the sprites. They chortled a joyful answer and then dissipated back into the currents, leaving the boat to drift as it would.

Reheuel collapsed to the ground and stretched out, reveling in the solid earth beneath his body. Ariel sighed. "I knew a time when such a little trip would barely have phased you."

Reheuel nodded as he searched through his pack. "Times change."

"I sometimes forget," Ariel replied. "Time changes so little in my city. What are thirty years? A pause in a conversation? For you they could be a lifetime."

"For many they are a lifetime," Reheuel replied. "I've been fortunate."

"It's so beautiful," Ariel said, her voice musing, abstract. "You have to fit so much into so little time. You have to love, to fight, to share, to cling, to punish, to forgive. You have to feel pride and shame and wonder and disgust. You have to love. All in the space of a fairy's laughter. It is beautiful that men find the time."

Reheuel sat up. "Do you miss it?" he asked.

"Miss what?"

"Death, I suppose. Do you miss knowing that each second only comes once?"

"Sometimes," Ariel replied. "But other times I fear death even in my current state. It would be so hard for me to die, but sometimes I awake in the night and scream, afraid that I might slip away in my sleep and lose everything I've worked for. I think of the centuries I have wasted, the time unimaginable ill spent and realize how I have wasted immortality. Then I fear its loss even more."

Reheuel stood. "Well, let's not waste any time then." He set off toward the mountain which rose a few miles off, carefully setting his boots against the oak roots and rocks that offered themselves on the upward trek.

Ariel followed about twenty feet above, watching the surrounding forests for movement. Every hour or so, as Reheuel climbed, Ariel descended and gave him instructions, leading him to the quickest paths, avoiding steeper inclines and shale.

The going was slow, and Reheuel paused often to rest. His legs burned beneath him, shin splints aching with every new step. But he continued, often hand over hand up the side of steep hills, tearing the flesh from his fingers and gouging the leather of his boots. When night fell, he slept in a flat wood, stretched out beneath a canopy of ferns.

* * *

On the second day of travel, Hefthon stopped at the edge of a forest to hunt. He formed snares from his spare bowstrings and searched for rabbit trails to set them over. Tressa and Veil gathered strawberries and early raspberries in the fields around the wood. Hefthon hated to leave them alone, but he knew that food was their primary concern. Hunger was a far more pressing danger than goblins.

He quietly stalked the woods for most of that day, hoping to find turkey, or perhaps a deer. In the evening, he returned to the camp with three squirrels and a rabbit from his snare. Nightfall found the game spitting grease over a small campfire.

Veil rocked on her heels a few feet off, staring into the fire. "Will they be all right, Hefthon?" she asked.

Hefthon smiled. "We've beaten the goblins before. I'm sure we can do it again. When we get home, they'll all be waiting there. Old Shoen will be sitting on his porch, barking at the children as they chase the carts bound for market. Kezeik will be drilling in the courtyard of the keep. Euri will be fighting with her customers in the market, squabbling over seeds and cloth. It'll be just like it was."

Tressa laid her hand on her son's shoulder and squeezed gently in thanks. Veil resumed staring into the fire, trying to put together another question. She could feel the burden of her city bearing down on her young shoulders, but her mind could scarcely process the true nature of its danger. The age-old war of youth raged within her, her heart yearning to tremble but her mind unable to process real fear.

Tressa sat down beside her son and passed him a rag full of berries. "Geuel will warn them," she whispered. "Don't worry for home."

Hefthon nodded. "It feels so wrong. I can see them all, all my friends, lining up to fight. Rishka and Toman with their axes and pitchforks and Hayden with his sling. They'll all be fighting. And I'll be here, safe and useless."

Tressa squeezed his hand. "Duty doesn't always bring glory. This is your duty. And not one man in Gath Odrenoch would ever doubt your desire to be there."

"Then why do I feel like I'm deserting them?" Hefthon asked. "I'm out here, leaving them to defend my home. They'll grow up together in one night, and years from now, around fires in the evening, they'll all say, 'Remember that night when the goblins attacked? Remember how . . .' And they'll remember together and be together, secure in a perfect knowledge of each other's mettle. And I'll be apart."

"Perhaps," Tressa replied. "But will that matter if you did your duty? Just because one task receives the glory does not mean that others should be left undone." Tressa pointed over at Veil, who was lying down now, staring at the stars.

"She is your duty. And as long as you do right by her, then no man in Gath Odrenoch will ever have just call to shame you."

Just then a glimmer of light flashed by above them. Veil sat up. "A fairy!" she cried.

Hefthon watched the light as it dipped down into the trees and paused on a branch. "They must be gathering again."

"Perhaps they're recovering," Tressa said. "Perhaps they can live without the Tear."

The three remained silent for several seconds as they watched the Fairy fly out of sight once more. For the rest of that evening, a strange peace filled each of them, a reassurance they could not put words to.

* * *

Within the fairy keep, a choir of voices, crystalline and ethereal, swelled and echoed in stone passages. With each passing second, new voices joined the song as fairies, unused to relying on their own volition, let the music draw them in.

Throughout the keep, in passages and rooms all around the central hall, the council members led the singing, their own voices stronger and lower than the others.

Randiriel floated in the center of the main hall and listened to the music, feeling her people growing stronger. The music was a mere triviality to her, a pleasantry. But to the other fairies, it was a decision, an action taken without another's direction. And each fairy that joined felt itself grow closer to the others singing, discovering the bonds of natural affection.

Beside Randiriel, another fairy floated, his gold clothing tinting his glow nearly as brightly as Randiriel's own. "We

have enough food for tomorrow," he said. "All of the
gatherers have returned."

Randiriel nodded. "Thank you, Rylen. How are they?"

"Stronger," he replied. "They're not children anymore.
None of us are."

"Take me to them," Randiriel said. She followed him
upward several levels and down the hall to the throne
room. About two hundred fairies were gathered there,
engaged variously. Some were sorting the food. Others
were talking. A number stood chattering excitedly by the
far wall, clustered around something not quite visible.

Randiriel approached these and floated over them to see
what they were discussing. A single fairy stood on the
ground with her hands pressed to the wall. A bright glow
shone from beneath her hands, filtering through the flesh
on her fingers and darkly shadowing the bones of her palm.
Her face was set and hard, her eyes closed in concentration.
Beneath her hands, the dull, rotting wall of the keep shone
bright silver, fresh and pure. Randiriel smiled. "Beautiful,"
she said.

The fairy opened her eyes and removed her hands from
the wall. The glow faded, and slowly the wall dulled, as if
the silver were melting into the surrounding rot. "It's like
before," she said excitedly. "I can still create."

"We all can," Randiriel said. She opened her hand, and
a tiny bluebarrel made of light sprouted from her palm,
shooting out leaves that draped from her palm and opening
its flower between her fingers. Randiriel looked up, and the
flower faded, turning to dust and sifting down to the floor.
"But not like before. Without the Tear, we are weaker." She
pointed to the now barely perceptible spot of silver on the
wall. "But we are still fairy."

Several of the other fairies began placing their hands on
the wall, struggling to rediscover their former strengths.
Some were rewarded by tiny glimmers of light. Most were

not. Soon, the other fairies around the room drew closer and began trying as well. Randiriel smiled as she watched them. They were growing. Even if the Tear was never reclaimed, this group would survive. This group would find a way.

Occasionally, she approached those that were struggling and tried to help, to explain. But words fell short of aid. Creating was like moving, like breathing. You merely did it. There was no process, no command. Just volition. Learning to create was like finding a new muscle.

All that night, the fairies worked in the throne room, struggling to rediscover their power. They seemed oblivious to all else, absorbed in the necessity of understanding their new lives. Occasionally Randiriel wondered how they would ever return to their old selves once the Tear was returned. Fairies could not work so hard, focus so long. How could this group ever forget their single-mindedness, the drive that now motivated them?

She cast the thought aside as trivial, trusting that Ariel would have the answers. Ariel always had the answers.

A hand alighted on her shoulder, and she turned to face one of the council members, a dark-haired female with a silver dress. "Brylle," Randiriel said with a smile, "what is it?"

Brylle pointed to the fairies fluttering around the walls, struggling to rebuild. "This isn't a good idea," she said. "They can't use the Tear."

"Neither can we," Randiriel replied. "Yet we're holding this entire building. They're growing—just like us."

"They can't though," Brylle replied. "They can't—be like us. Do you want them to never go back?"

"I want them to go forward. To learn."

"They'll fall," Brylle said softly, "just like you fell. They'll learn too much to ever be innocent again. And even the Tear won't save them. They'll be trapped—like this."

Randiriel looked over at the glowing walls, at the faces
of the fairies that worked there. Their eyes were flashing
with knowledge, with thought. A haze that had always
seemed to veil their features was gone. "Well, maybe *this*
isn't so bad," Randiriel replied. "I feel fine."

"That's because you're not like them," Brylle said.
"You've never been like them. You're stronger, already past
innocence. The children who become fairies, they're the
weakest, the most fragile. If you try to make them like us,
they won't survive."

"If the Tear isn't found," Randiriel replied, "what then?
Will they be better off as children?"

"No, no they won't."

Randiriel nodded. "Then let them learn."

* * *

The heavy scent of flowering valerian filled Geuel's
nostrils as he half-trotted, half-staggered through the plains
below the Blue Hills. The tall, white flowers clustered
thickly all around him. Often, he bent to pull his feet from
under them, long since exhausted with snapping their
strong stalks. His chaps were stained deep green, and the
tiny white flowers filled every crevice of his clothing. Their
fresh scent had been invigorating at first, a refreshing
change from the smell of pine sap and moldering forest. But
now it was sickening, heavy and full. Geuel had long since
tied his handkerchief around his face, trying to get a breath
of clean, unscented air. His lungs burned with exertion, and
his legs ached.

One more day, he kept telling himself, one more day.
He knew that sometime the following night he would reach
Gath Odrenoch, and there would be warm water and clean
bandages and a real bed. He glanced down at his arm
where he had cut himself on the sword. The wound was
closed but already discolored. The scabs were blackish and
covered in grime. His sweat ran muddily over the surface

of the wound. Soon he would be facing serious trouble if he couldn't get it cleaned.

When he reached the edge of the Blue Hills in the early afternoon, he rested on the brow of the first and ate. The short grass and squat bluebarrels were a welcome change from the field grass and valerians of the plain. His water was nearly gone, but several streams ran through the Blue Hills, some of the Faeja's many tributaries between the Gath mountains and Elicathaliss. The rest of his food would last him for the journey. Hefthon's pack had paid off.

As he ate, he stared off at the Gath mountains. He could see the first few peaks clearly from where he sat. The others were shrouded in mist and cloud. The first mountains of the Gath chain were relatively small. Stark and intimidating in appearance but almost childish compared to the later peaks. Geuel wondered how far his father would have to climb, whether he would have to face the farther heights. Either way, the task was insanity.

He ate slowly, allowing himself a rare rest before starting again. He regretted it as soon as he stood. His legs, already aching, felt as stiff as boards. Each step sent a jolt through his shins that terminated sharply in his knees. The pain was becoming unbearable.

He was nearing the end of the Blue Hills when night fell. It was cold, colder with no trees or vegetation to block the wind. He shivered for several hours before finally drifting into a shaky sleep. Once more, dreams haunted him. He saw Gath Odrenoch burning, his people dying. But now he was merely an observer, detached from the events themselves. His location changed with the progression of the dream, fluctuating between the Gath mountains and the city. He saw his father, trapped and struggling in a cave, overpowered by a mass of writhing creatures—goblins but changed, stronger and larger. He saw the Blue Hills and Hefthon left alone protecting his mother and sister, failing and dying. In the distance, smoke rose from somewhere. And though he couldn't see it, he knew that it was the last remnant of the fairy city—burning. And where was he? Where was Geuel? Trapped, somewhere between. He alone was safe and secure. He couldn't protect any of them.

He awoke on the fourth morning, cold but somehow still covered in sweat. Thick clouds blotted out the eastern horizon where he knew the sun was already rising. The air smelled of rain.

* * *

Reheuel awoke on the third day to the whistle of a silver byrce. The large bird sat preening itself in the boughs of a gnarled oak jutting out from the edge of a nearby cliff. Ariel was already awake. She sat still on a milkweed plant, caressing the back of a monarch caterpillar. Reheuel watched her for a few seconds. Before the boat ride, he had never seen a fairy so still before. They were always dashing and flitting about, ever in the bustle and hurry of youth. Even when they sat in one place, they trembled constantly, as if all their energy were struggling for an outlet. Between their constant movement and the bright light that emanated from their bodies, it was rare to see them in detail.

Ariel wasn't like the other fairies though. She moved with a kind of gravity, slow and dignified. And as she sat on the milkweed plant, her calm dimmed the light within her. She looked almost human aside from her size. She had pale white skin and dark black hair. Her build was slight, like all of her kind. But at that moment, there was nothing childish in her appearance, nothing fantastic or magical. She was simply a tiny woman with transparent wings.

Reheuel felt vaguely puzzled by her appearance. She was, in every respect aside from size, what one would call beautiful. In fact, all of the fairies were beautiful. And yet he could not imagine anyone finding Ariel "attractive." It was as if her people held the beauty of art, something as distinct from fleshly beauty as the beauty of a sunrise.

Even Ariel, a fallen fairy who lacked the twinkling eyes and eternal laughter of youth, was so detached from humanity's pains and pleasures that her very beauty took on the hue of the unnatural.

She looked over at Reheuel and nodded to the mountain. "Ready to start?" she asked.

"Guess it doesn't really matter," he replied, lifting the pack he had been using as a pillow and strapping it back into place.

Ariel rose and stroked the caterpillar one last time as if in farewell and then flashed upward several feet, her light burning brighter with the exertion of her wings. She pointed to the cliff where the oak tree hung twenty feet above. "We'll head up here," she said.

Reheuel laughed. "Not all of us have wings, and I'm not climbing shale."

"You won't have to," Ariel replied and approached the cliff. She extended one hand and clenched it tightly, grinding her fist until it burned too brightly to look at. A set of six stairs, shimmering with an internal sunlight, materialized in front of her, stretching upward toward the cliff.

Reheuel glanced at them uncertainly. "You're sure you can hold them?" he asked.

"No," Ariel replied, "but no one lives forever."

Reheuel laughed as he stepped onto the stairs. "Easy for you to say."

He climbed steadily, struggling to keep his eyes trained in front of him. But even without looking down, he could feel the lighting change as the stairs behind him dissipated and new ones flickered to life in front of him. They felt brittle and smooth, like walking on glass. And the slower he walked, the more he felt that they might crack beneath his weight. By the time he reached the top, he was nearly running, the stairs evaporating as soon as he left them and appearing beneath his already falling feet. He tumbled to the top of the cliff and lay face down, grasping clumps of field grass to assure his body that he was on solid ground again.

Ariel landed beside his head and pointed upward to another cliff face. "Let's keep moving," she said.

Reheuel pushed himself to his feet and approached the new cliff face. "All right, I'm ready."

After he reached the top of the second cliff, Reheuel stopped and looked back at Ariel. She looked dimmer, her glow pale and faded. "You alright?" he asked.

She shook her head and landed on his shoulder. "Your turn to carry," she said. Her skin was waxy and stretched, and tendrils of gray threaded through her hair.

"You going to be able to keep this up?" he asked.

"I'll be fine," she said. "Just—tired."

He set off to the north at a brisk hike, and Ariel wound herself into the rawhide straps on top of his backpack, settling down to rest. When he looked back down the mountain later in the afternoon, he realized that Ariel's stairs had saved him hours of hiking.

They spent the rest of that day traveling over the first of the Gath mountains, crossing it about halfway up. Occasionally, Ariel would build stairs or a rope or some other temporary construct to help Reheuel avoid detours or tiring climbs. But most of the day she simply slept on the backpack, exhausted by the use of her power.

When night fell, it found them on the far side of the first mountain, resting in a pass at the base of two twin peaks. Ariel pointed to the westernmost of the two. "The caves start about halfway up. We should make it by nightfall tomorrow."

Reheuel nodded as he dug up a root with his knife. "Yeah, I remember. You going to be all right tomorrow?"

Ariel looked down at her hands. Even in the darkness of the evening, her light was faint and flickering. Her hair had lost its youthful gloss, and a shock of gray ran back from her right brow. "I'll be fine. I can feel my Tear up there," she said, nodding to the mountain. "I can feel its power."

Reheuel cut the root away and lay down. "Good, then we didn't waste a trip."

Ariel glanced around at the scraggly woods that surrounded them. "We should keep watch," she said. "I'll go first."

Reheuel nodded. "Wake me in a few hours."

* * *

On the third morning, Hefthon woke before the sunrise. The air smelled of valerians from the fields around them, and he breathed deeply to shake off the drowsiness of the night. Two squirrels still hung over the dirt-covered embers. He slid them off of the skewer and wrapped them into his pack. At least they'd have something to tide them over for the day. He packed up what items they had in the camp and then gently shook Veil and Tressa. "Time to move," he said softly. "Sun's almost up."

They ate quickly, finishing off the last of the bread and some leftover rabbit. Then they left. Hefthon led the way, following the trail left by Geuel. It was easy to find in the fields: beaten grass and broken plant stalks abounded. In the woods though, he often lost it and made his own paths.

By mid-afternoon, he found himself stopping periodically to wait for Veil. The girl was strong, but she had never traveled far on foot, and she struggled to match her brother's long strides. With each new stop, Hefthon felt a little more of his temper ground away. He wished that he could have switched places with Geuel, that he could be the one already nearing Gath Odrenoch. He fingered the pommel of his sword often and imagined himself lined with the other guards, waiting behind the parapet, watching goblin campfires in the distance.

Each minute that passed pulled him that much farther away from any chance at glory. He felt shamed, cut off from the world he belonged to. "Hurry up!" he called over his shoulder, watching Veil stumble through a stand of blackberry canes. At any other time, he would have regretted the words, but at that moment his sister scarcely mattered. What mattered was Gath Odrenoch. And Veil was robbing him of his only chance to defend it.

Tressa glanced sharply at her son, but she remained silent. She saw his hands, fumbling agitatedly with his sword handle. She saw the stoop to his back and the spring-wound tension in his movements. She knew that his mental anguish was just as acute as his sister's exhaustion. One was worn by travel, the other by rest. But both were nearly broken.

They made camp beneath a stand of tag alder, partially sheltered from a cold wind that had sprung up in the evening. Hefthon handed his sword to Tressa and moved toward the edge of camp. "I'll start hunting in the evenings," he said, "save us the need for extra stops."

"Don't exhaust yourself," she said.

Hefthon nodded. "I won't. I have too much energy anyway."

Chapter 8

The sun rose dully on the fourth morning. From her perch on the roof of the fairy keep, Randiriel could just make out its hazy outline behind a bank of thick gray storm clouds. It rose slowly from the eastern horizon, its dim light seeping over the forests like a stain. The eastern side of the Faeja was darker and wilder than the western, heavy with hundreds of miles of forest. It was all, technically, under the Iris. But the lands to the east held no real allegiance to man. They were the forests of the elves and the gnomes, steeped in ancient allegiances and enchantments far predating any single empire. As the sun climbed, the forests shed their deeper shadows, lit with a pallid gray. Their leaves took on the muted colors of an old painting. To the distant northeast, Randiriel thought she could see the gleam of Lake Esrathel, home of the merpeople.

When the light of dawn finally struck the Faeja, the sun had nearly risen; it devoured the plains beyond rapidly. Randiriel turned and watched as gray chased black across the plains of the human empire, swallowing the scattered woodlands and miles of farmland in dreary daylight. She knew that somewhere, miles beyond the horizon, lay the mighty Western Mountains, the true end of the Iris's dominion. And somewhere between those distant rocks and the river which flowed beside Randiriel's keep lay the Capital, the center of human order, the Crystal City.

There's a flag out there somewhere, a golden iris sown in sky-blue silk.

That's what Geuel had said. Randiriel scoured the plains with her eyes, knowing that the Capital was beyond the horizon but still wishing she could see its distant sparkle. She wondered what it would be like, to believe in a symbol so purely that you would die for it. She pictured herself as a woman, as if she had never become a fairy. She thought of living in the Capital, walking beneath that banner every day and knowing that it was her own. The fantasy was nearly intoxicating. To live every day with a fear of impending death, to spend every moment as if it might be your last, to know that your life was as brief as a winter breath.

Perhaps that was why the humans loved their symbol. The symbol was a taste of eternity. Every human was born to die, but the Iris never had to. The Iris could go on and on through the ages. And when a man gave to the Iris, his gift lasted.

Every one of them would bleed again, just to see it wave where it has never waved before.

Randiriel smiled to herself. She would see the Golden Iris. She would watch it wave above the Crystal City and try to believe. She looked down at the dull silver of the fairy keep. The Fairy City had been beautiful. But trivial. Temporary as childhood. While Ariel had meant it to last forever, it had passed in a matter of days. And even if it was never reborn, its passing would change nothing in the world. Its only meaning was in novelty.

A distant peal of thunder rumbled in the east, nipping the heels of an unseen lightning bolt. Randiriel glanced in that direction and saw the black centers of the gray clouds churning angrily. The storm would be brutal. A flash of silver off to her left made her turn her head. Brylle landed on the roof nearby and nodded toward the storm clouds. "The others will be frightened," she said. "They've never felt a storm alone."

"They'll live. It's only sound."

"Perhaps, but not to children," she replied. "To children, it's the sound of Ingway, clapping his wings as he comes for their souls."

Randiriel laughed. "We're not children, Brylle. Most of us have lived through five generations. It's time we all grew up."

"Many have," Brylle replied, "thanks to you. But the others need care."

"Then care for them," Randiriel replied. "What difference does it make though, whether their fantasy shatters now or a thousand years from now? Someday, their constructed innocence will end, and they will face the same world that every grown being faces, a world with pain and anger and costly beauty. And nothing will have changed for their extended innocence. Nothing to last."

"But at least they'll have that thousand years," Brylle said. She paused for a moment. "You're not going back, are you?"

Randiriel shook her head. "Ariel told me as much, though I think she meant to hide it. Not that it matters. I'm glad. I want to leave—to feel and to know. I want to see the Iris waving over the Capital."

Brylle sat down and stared out with her over the plains. "I've lived for a long time, Rand," she said. "I've seen the world and known it."

"Then how can you stay here?"

"Because beauty has no cost here," Brylle said. "And you're right, every childhood we save will eventually shatter, no matter what Ariel may wish to the contrary. But at least they will make the world beautiful a little while longer. I think that means something. Perhaps, after you leave here and see the world's pain, then you will see why this place matters."

Randiriel smiled doubtfully. "Perhaps," she said and went back to watching the plains.

* * *

The rain began shortly after noon, soft and pleasant at first, tiny droplets floating on a cooling breeze. They soothed the burning in Geuel's arm where his wound still festered. Gradually though, the sprinkling became a downpour, the droplets swelling to bulbous proportions and growing in number till they felt like one solid mass of lukewarm water.

Geuel opened his mouth periodically to refresh himself, still enjoying the rain as a welcome change from his journey's usual swelter. It slowed him down, but he knew that he could still make the city by nightfall.

By mid-afternoon though, the rain had shifted from a welcome relief to an extreme inconvenience. The water, which had initially felt almost warm, chilled as Geuel's body grew accustomed to it. In less than an hour, it felt freezing. Several times he fell while struggling up muddy hills and embankments. And each time he found it harder to rise again. Bruises and scrapes previously forgotten became more sensitive as the water ran down through his clothing and soaked at dried scabs and dirt. His body grew cramped and stiff. When evening neared, his visibility was gone, particularly in the woodlands. If his surroundings had not already become familiar, he knew that he would never have found his way. Around five thirty, he reached one of the outlying farms and struggled over the wooden fence of its pasture. He threw aside his pack about halfway across the field, welcoming even that tiny loss of weight.

When he reached the house, the full exhaustion of his journey came crashing down on him all at once. Every mile, forced from his mind by necessity, suddenly made itself known in his groaning joints. The torn blisters on his already calloused feet screamed in the stinging water that filled his boots.

He pounded on the door with his right hand, letting his left drop to his thigh to support his drooping body.

The door creaked open partway, and a boy around Hefthon's age peered out cautiously. He swung the door open when he recognized Geuel. "Geuel!" he cried, "what are you doing out in this infernal weather? Come in."

Geuel pulled himself upright by the door frame and entered. "Thanks, Toman," he said. "Listen, I've come from the Fairy City."

Toman started to laugh, knowing Geuel's disdain for the little people. His laugh died on his lips as Geuel gripped his collar.

"Listen," Geuel said, his voice coming in a pained growl, "the goblins are coming. The Fairy City's gone, collapsed into the Faeja."

Toman paled and dragged Geuel farther inside. "Talk to my parents," he said. "Tell them everything. I'll ride for the city."

Geuel shook his head. "I'll go."

"You can barely stand," Toman replied. "Stay here. Follow when you can."

Geuel nodded. "Thank you, Toman."

Toman grabbed a coat from a nearby rack and darted outside, his eyes flashing with excitement. Geuel closed the door behind him and sat down to take off his shoes. Toman's father and sister entered from the dining room nearby.

"Geuel, what happened to you, boy?" Toman's father asked, glancing at the door from which his son had just left.

"Goblins," Geuel replied. "Toman's gone to warn the city."

A short while later, Geuel sat in a rocking chair in the family's living room, washed and dressed in some of Toman's clothes. Even unlaced at the throat, the shirt bulged uncomfortably on Geuel's large frame. But it felt good to be clean.

Toman's father listened quietly as Geuel told his story, pausing afterward to consider. After a moment, he said, "There's no doubt they'll come. They've been feeling us out all summer, prowling the farmland. I know at least half a dozen folks who've seen 'em skulking 'bout their farms in the evenings. We'll head for town, get behind the walls with the others. We can warn the Perring farm on the way. No doubt they'll send out riders to warn the others."

Geuel stood, his joints groaning in protest. "You should bring food, weapons. It may be days before they show, may be hours."

"Goblins aren't known for planning," Toman's father replied. "If they have a weapon, I doubt they'll wait to use it." He turned back to his daughter. "Saddle four horses," he said. "Make sure the others can get out to pasture."

"What should I do?" Geuel asked.

Toman's father hooked his hand. "Come on to the cellar with me, I've got some things to fetch." He walked over to the kitchen and dragged aside the main table. An iron ring lay set into the wood beneath it. Toman's father dragged up on it and pulled part of the floor free, sliding it aside. A dark hole yawned in its place, a flight of rough-hewn wooden stairs running down into the darkness.

Lifting a tallow candle from its niche in the wall, Toman's father moved down into the darkness. Geuel followed and found himself in a small cellar, roughly the size of the kitchen above them. Wooden shelves lined one wall, covered in clay pots and glass jars of canned produce. Against the other wall lay a few cedar chests. Above them, wooden pegs jutted from the wall with two leather cuirasses. Toman's father opened the cedar chests and handed off the contents to Geuel: two plain swords, a dagger, an old wooden shield, and a bow with twelve arrows. He pointed to the stairs. "Take that lot to the horses. I'll fetch what's left." He dragged the armor sets from the wall and began piling jars of produce into them.

Geuel strode quickly outside where he found the girl and Toman's mother cinching the saddles of several large plow horses. He strapped the swords into place on two saddles and hung the dagger on his belt. The shield, he tied into place with a strip of leather from Toman's sister and the bow and arrows he rolled into a pack using a blanket from Toman's mother.

Within twenty minutes, the four of them were riding for Gath Odrenoch. Every few minutes, Geuel looked upward to the skyline, waiting for the orange glow of fire over the trees, waiting for his nightmares to come true.

* * *

Reheuel awoke on the fourth morning to a chilling wind. The mountains of Gath were small, but the air was still cold at the height where he lay. He struggled upright and stretched his back with a grunt, feeling his body settle its members back into place after another night on lumpy earth. Ariel flew down from the bough of a nearby stunted poplar. "Are you ready to climb?" she asked.

Reheuel nodded. "Last day, why not?"

They traveled in silence for most of that morning, the cold filling them both with a sense of apprehension. Dark clouds hung brooding over the eastern sky, and far off in the distance, Reheuel could see the trailing curtains of a distant rainfall. It reached them just before noon, a miserable downpour that soaked the rocks and turned every minor cliff face into a death trap.

Ariel flew low, buffeted by the rain drops that, to her, felt like waves. She seldom created any aids for Reheuel, her focus constantly shattered by the storm. Several times, she crawled beneath shelves of rock or pine boughs to rest her wings from the weight of the water. And each time, it only became harder to fly after she had moved on.

Reheuel struggled as he climbed, falling twice when his hands slipped on the wet rock of small cliffs. His arms and waist were bruised heavily by the time they stopped to eat midway through the day. Ariel curled up beneath the shelter of a group of ferns and tried to blot out the sounds of the storm. "How much farther?" she called over the wind.

Reheuel shrugged. "A few hours normally, but probably not till nightfall in this."

"Should we wait till morning?" Ariel asked. "They'll be more active in the night."

Reheuel glanced about at their surroundings. They were in a small hollow, blocked from the wind by a rise to the east and sheltered partially from the rain by the poplar trees that surrounded them. "Perhaps, this is as good a place as any to stop."

He unrolled his wool blanket and dragged himself back against the base of a poplar tree, feeling the trickles of rain that burst through the thin branches and ran down onto his shoulders. It was going to be a long and miserable rest. He never noticed, hours later, when exactly he fell asleep. But he awoke with a start in the night. Ariel stood on his shoulder, tugging at his sleeve frantically. "Look," she hissed as his eyes struggled open.

He turned sharply to follow her pointing arm and gasped. It was night, and the rain had stopped. The moon and stars were completely hidden by the thick clouds overhead, but still hundreds of lights glowed above them in the night sky, drifting westward like a cloud of embers from a forest fire. "Fairies?" he asked, knowing the answer but unable to imagine any other explanation.

Ariel shook her head. "Our light is clean, like sunlight."

He looked again at the cloud that still drifted overhead, at least three hundred strong now, several hundred feet up and spread out in a wild spray. The light was orange and hazy, like embers clouded in smoke and ash. It flickered and shifted in intensity like a dying fire.

"What are they then?" he asked.

Ariel's eyes were wide and gleamed in the darkness. Her body trembled with fear and offense. It was the most emotional Reheuel had ever seen her. "Something new," she whispered, "something horrible and new."

"You don't mean they're—"

"They *were* goblins," Ariel replied. "I'm afraid they're something else entirely now."

"Gath Odrenoch," Reheuel whispered, "they'll be there before morning."

"We have to find the Tear," Ariel said. "It will not stop them, but at least it will weaken them."

Reheuel packed his blanket quickly and dragged his pack over his shoulders. "We're leaving now," he said. "We can't wait any longer."

Ariel shook the moisture from her wings and flew upward a few feet. The cloud had passed now and was moving off to the west, a sea of glowing lights that winked and guttered in the darkness. A smell of ash drifted over Ariel and Reheuel. Their eyes stung as if from smoke.

They moved off together up the mountain side. The ground was still wet, but much of the excess water had run off down the mountain face and the going was faster. Ariel occasionally stopped to provide steps.

Midway through their trip, Reheuel noticed a light filling the southern sky. He thought at first that the clouds had cleared. Instead of the moon though, he saw another cloud of lights filling the sky, white and beautiful and clean. They shone like tiny suns, as alive and constant as their celestial counterpart. Reheuel wondered briefly how he could have ever mistaken the ember light of the goblins for these clean creatures.

Ariel gasped. "My children," she said, "where are they going?"

"Looks like north," Reheuel replied.

"The goblins," Ariel said. She instinctively moved toward the light, protective and afraid. "They're going after the goblins."

Reheuel shook his head. "They couldn't. They were broken without the Tear."

"Rand could," Ariel replied. "If she made the others . . ."

"They'll die," Reheuel finished, letting his eyes fall to the ground at his feet.

"Yes," Ariel said, "and if they live, then what will they be? Without innocence, they will not be fairy. They will never reconnect to the Tear. They will be—"

"Outcasts."

Ariel sank down to her knees on the earth, staring at the lights, the brave little lights flying to the north. Her eyes closed, and she let her hands fall folded between her legs. And, once more, if fairies could weep.

After several hours, they neared a group of cave mouths. There were rough timber walls blocking these openings and gates with iron studs. But no visible sentries stood astride the walls, and no movement showed around them. Only the sounds of running water echoed from behind each gate.

Ariel peered cautiously around the trunk of the birch tree she stood behind. "See if you can get closer," she said to Reheuel. "They may have all left."

Reheuel nodded and slipped out into the open, crouched down in the shallow bell heather. His bow was out now, strung and nocked with a broad tipped arrow. His feet made almost no noise as they softly brushed the heather flowers. He reached the wall undetected and placed his ear to the wood. Again, he heard rushing water but nothing else. He studied the wall above for movement and carefully checked each visible arrow loop. But no movement caught his eye. He waved to Ariel to come forward. If there were any guards, they could hardly help but notice her glowing figure.

She landed on the ground beside him and looked up the nine-foot palisades. "Use these," she whispered and placed her hand on the wall. Along its face, tiny pegs of solid light, just large enough for Reheuel to grasp, jutted out evenly. Reheuel hung his bow around his body and quickly pulled himself up the palisade, slipping quietly over the far side. He rested silently on the wall's upper walkway and peered into the cave, his first true look at the goblin world.

The three cave mouths all opened into the same room, a massive hall-like structure filled with low stone barracks and stables. He could smell the stables and the rank odor of whatever creatures were kept inside. About halfway across the hall, he saw the gleam of water. A narrow river flowed across the cavern in a semicircle, its outer loop toward the wall on which Reheuel rested. The cave into which the river flowed seemed to be the only entrance further into the mountain. Ariel flew up beside him and sniffed the air. "I don't think there's anything here," she said.

Reheuel nodded and approached some nearby stairs. They were too narrow for his feet, and he had to walk sideways as he climbed down. His long strides skipped over four steps at a time. Ariel flew down beside him and pointed to the river. "I guess that's our route," she said.

A small bridge extended over the stream, wide enough for three to walk abreast but with no rails or walls. It hung just inches over the surface of the water, and beneath it an iron grill descended into the water. A stack of roughly carved poles lay on the bridge, and a dozen or so tiny canoes floated to the left, bumping softly against the iron grill. Reheuel walked out and lifted one of these canoes, dragging it over to the other side where it could run with the current. Ariel landed in it as he stepped down and shuddered as her feet settled in a layer of slime. "We should land as soon as possible," she said.

Reheuel nodded. "I'd hate to be caught on the water if they find us."

He stood in the center of the canoe and punted it along with the current, shaking occasionally as he struggled to maintain his footing. The canoe rode dangerously low under his weight, its walls just two inches above the water level.

"Look at the banks," Ariel said as they rode.

Reheuel glanced at them. They were steep and straight, unnaturally angular. "They were carved," he said. "These streams must be like roads."

When the canoe entered the dark mouth of the exit, Reheuel stowed his pole on the floor of the canoe, its end hanging out on the right side, and unslung his bow. The new cave was little more than a tunnel, a long, narrow hole lit only by Ariel's glow. On the walls, strange carvings flickered in the dim light, ancient monsters and creatures with names lost even to legend, remembered only in the hereditary fears of the goblins. Several times, as they rode, Reheuel thought he saw these carvings move. But each time he attributed it to the poor lighting and the shifting shadows.

The ride through the tunnel lasted for about twenty minutes, and then a light appeared at the mouth of an exit. It looked like neither sunlight nor daylight; it was duller, pale blue in tone. At first Reheuel thought it might be starlight, for it carried an oldness and a grayness. But it was too dim for starlight, too lackluster. This light was not so much old as sickly.

Reheuel tensed and lifted his bow in anticipation as they entered the light, but almost immediately he realized how useless the motion was. Moving from the pitch of the tunnel into this new light blinded him, causing him to

quickly swing an arm over his eyes. He overturned the
canoe as he did so, slipping off and crashing into the cold,
four-foot water. Ariel shot upward immediately and hung
above the water, staring in wonder at the world around
them. For it was a world. The words hall and cavern fall
desperately short of describing the true expanse of the area
they had entered. It was conical in shape, as if the entire
mountain were merely a hollow shell or an immensely
thick wall. On its sides, from the floor around her and
upwards for half a mile, thick, phosphorescent blue moss
clustered like matted grass. It lit the entire expanse as far as
she could see.

Towers and castles carved from the living rock of the
mountain rose upward haphazardly yet majestically, the
handiwork of centuries of labor. The angles were rough and
ragged, the walls unpolished. Yet the overall effect of a city
built from one stone was staggering. Many buildings had
the melted look of stalagmites, covered in the residue of a
thousand years of dripping water. Others had channels
carved into their roofs and running down their bases
toward the stream, single-droplet rivers carved by time.

And amidst all the grotesque splendor, the city was
silent. No guttural nickers rattled from the open doors, no
mealy howls from the towers overhead. The city might
have been abandoned for centuries to judge by the sounds.
Only the smell assured Ariel that goblins did indeed dwell
in this place, the sickly, heavy scent of habitation and
refuse, rotting flesh from scrap piles and rotting feces from
some distant sewage system.

Reheuel clambered to shore and grunted in anger,
clutching his leg. A long, thin lamprey clung doggedly to
his leather chaps, struggling to break through to his flesh.
Reheuel stabbed it with his dagger and flicked it back into
the water. The surface roiled briefly as some larger shape
moved in, drawn by the blood in the water.

He stood and looked around at the city that surrounded them. It went on for miles, far beyond where his gaze ended. The far wall above the city was merely a hazy patch of light, like the sky from the earth above. "Which way?" he asked Ariel, the sound of dripping from his soaked clothing amplified in the silence and stone.

Ariel pointed toward the center of the city. "That way," she said.

Reheuel nodded, studying the towering keep that rose about half a mile distant, at least twice the height of any other building. "Guess it's pretty safe to guess which building?" he asked.

Chapter 9

Tat—tat—tat . . . The rain dulled to a thin staccato on the roof of the fairy keep, and around the main hall, fairies crept from their crevices to revel in their freedom from thunder. Randiriel watched them with a vague sense of disdain. She hated herself for the feeling, hated herself for so quickly condemning what she had only recently been. But the knowledge of her own prior weakness only increased her disgust. As the other fairies began to laugh and sing once more, she left, flying out to the roof to watch the rain clouds thin.

It was late, and the sky overhead was dark save for a few tiny gaps in the cloud cover where stars dared to peek through at the world below. The mountains of Gath were visible in the distance, darker pyramids in a sea of near-black. Randiriel loved the sky. It was one of the few traits she remembered sharing with the other fairies. They all loved to watch the sky. Only now did Randiriel begin to understand why even this similarity had in some ways set her apart.

The others had loved the sky for seeing it, enjoyed it as it was given to them. They watched the sunset, tasted the rain, and felt the wind as it played in their hair. They seemed so content with experience as it came, so naturally receptive to the bounds of their five senses. But Randiriel longed for something more from the sky, from the dim shapes on the horizon. She wanted to experience beyond sight and hearing and touch, beyond smell and taste. She wanted to wrap together all of those experiences at once and somehow be one with what she saw. When seized with these desires, she would often fly out into the clouds or valleys she was watching, flash as fast as she could from point to point and take it all in at once, every detail of sensation that her body gave her. But even this fell short of truly *experiencing* what she saw.

Was this what it meant to be real, to be haunted by a phantom desire for more than what was immediately real, to be ever in need of something further? Or had it been only an aberration, a symptom of discontent with her lot as a fairy? She knew that it could not be the latter. For, as she stared out at the night sky, already matured past her idyllic fairyhood, she still felt that haunting need for more.

She sat for several hours on the roof, watching the still forms of the Gath mountains in the distance. She wondered how Ariel was faring there, how close she was to regaining the Tear. Then her thoughts turned to the west of the mountains, to Gath Odrenoch where the Iris flew, and she thought of Geuel and wondered whether he had reached his precious city. Just then a flutter of wings sounded above and Brylle landed beside her. "Thought you'd be up here," she said.

Randiriel nodded. "Quiet is hard to find below."

They sat silent for several minutes, just watching the slow dissipation of the clouds. Then Randiriel pointed toward the Gath mountains. "What's that?" she asked, "do you see it?"

Brylle nodded. "Lights of some sort. They're coming out of the mountain. Surely not a fire?"

Randiriel shook her head. "No, they're . . . flying, I think. They look almost like," she paused, struggling to find another comparison but failing, "fairies."

Brylle shuddered, an unnatural revulsion coming over her at the comparison. She could barely see the distant cloud of lights, and she could definitely not identify them. But somehow the comparison still struck her as wrong, as twisted and vulgar. "Surely not," she said. "They're all below."

"The Tear," Randiriel said suddenly, "what else could it be?"

Brylle felt her stomach churn. "You think the goblins—"

"They're headed north. The only city there is Gath Odrenoch," Randiriel said, leaping off the roof and flying back down toward one of the windows, calling over her shoulder, "Round up the council members and gatherers. Meet me in the throne room."

Randiriel spent the next half hour racing through the halls and corridors of the keep, seeking out every fairy who had shown independence. When she finally reached the throne room, about four hundred fairies had gathered there, all whispering excitedly among themselves in tense anticipation. Brylle sat, ashen and pale, with the rest of the council members in their thrones. Randiriel ignored the thrones and stepped in front of the assembled fairies, raising her hands for silence.

"Brothers and sisters," she said, "listen to me. In the last few days, we have learned many things. We have traded the innocence of childhood for understanding. We have discovered self and free will and pain. But tonight, we must learn something new. We must learn to fight."

Behind Randiriel, several council members stood to their feet. "Silence!" cried one, a tall male fairy in a silver tunic. "Randiriel, Ariel told you to care for our people. But you overstep your authority. We are born of the Tear, and our people live through the cyntras of Innocence. They cannot fight. It violates their nature."

Randiriel turned on him. "The Tear is gone!" she cried, "And yet here we stand, all of us. We are more than simply vessels of the Tear's power. We are complete in ourselves. And I believe we can do as we will with the power we have left."

A female council member spoke. "All of you who do this, you sacrifice all hope of becoming one with the Tear again. You will be alone. Forever."

Rylen, the fairy in gold, stepped toward Randiriel. "I don't want to go back anyway," he said. "I don't want to forget. I'll follow you, Rand."

Randiriel turned to the others. "And you?" she asked. "I saw a cloud of lights tonight, like our own in migration. But they were darker and foul, headed for Gath Odrenoch. The goblins have taken our power, our very form, and now turn that form against our friends. Reheuel and his sons bled to protect us. We owe them our aid. And if not them, we owe ourselves. Do you not want vengeance for our fallen brethren?"

The male council member clutched a staff of light now, formed inside his hand. He slammed it down upon the floor and silenced the crowd of fairies with a deafening boom. "We have no ties to the outer world," he said. "We cannot afford to form them now. What happens in the world of men is the business of men."

"And what happens when that business is finished?" Randiriel asked. "What happens when the last of the men in Gath Odrenoch die? Will the goblins fly back to their caves and cower once more? They've attacked us once. They will finish the task. Let us unite with man while we can. If not for honor, then for survival. Perhaps none of you here care for man or the Iris. But I know you all love the City of Youth. For the hope of her restoration, join me."

Brylle stepped down from her throne and stood beside Randiriel. "I will fly with you," she said. "Those creatures are a mockery of all that the Tear preserves."

Seeing one of the council members with Randiriel, several more fairies stepped forward. Gradually, as the group increased in size, more began to step forward. And finally, all but a few dozen of the fairies in the room had joined Randiriel. She turned to Brylle and Rylen. "Thank you," she said.

Rylen placed a hand on her shoulder. "You set us free," he said, "and we do this freely."

"See you both after," Randiriel said. "Perhaps after tonight there will be time for brighter things."

"There's a whole world out there to see now," Rylen said, "and where's the joy in seeing it alone?"

Moments later, the windows of the fairy keep glowed as hundreds of tiny suns filtered out into the night. The dew on the fields glistened beneath their sunlight, and dozens of small night creatures scurried for cover away from their effulgence. Occasionally brighter glints flashed about these suns as fairies practiced forming weapons. Spears of light and silver daggers glittered in their fists as they flew, their eyes filled with a noble fear. For the first time since Ariel's Tear struck the Faeja, the fairies were going to war.

* * *

Hefthon woke to the smell of ashy smoke, the kind of smoke that curls from a bed of dying embers doused in water. He sat up quickly and searched the woods around him, his first thought flying to a forest fire. But the ground was still soaked. Water squelched in his woolen blanket as he turned, and he shivered with the chill of his wet shirt. The woods were dark and silent save for the drip of water from heavy branches.

He sniffed again, wondering if the scent had been some clinging remnant of a dream. But still his nostrils burned with ash. He looked upward then and saw them, hundreds of orange lights flickering in the darkness about fifty feet above. They were too far distant for him to see them clearly. Most merely looked like glowing embers. Several, however, held grotesque forms in their light, dark shadows of long-limbed figures. They hissed and winked as they struck moisture and straggling raindrops in the air. All of them, even the brightest, were wreathed in a kind of haze, as if half their composition were a cloud of smoke.

Hefthon crawled over to Veil and placed a hand over her mouth. She awoke with a start but remained silent, her eyes turning wildly in fear. Hefthon placed a finger to his lips and nodded upwards. Veil rolled over to look at the sky, and Hefthon released her. He crawled over to Tressa and gently shook her awake. Together, the three of them lay and watched the passing lights.

"What are they?" Veil whispered.

"I don't know," Hefthon replied. "Goblins maybe? Ariel never said what the Tear would do."

Tressa nudged Hefthon into silence, and they lay quiet till the lights had passed over. After the last fiery glow had disappeared, she turned to her son. "How long did Geuel say it would take him to reach home?"

"He should be there already," Hefthon replied, squeezing her hand. "I'm sure they'll be fine."

Tressa nodded. "Well, I'm not sleeping again tonight. We should get moving."

Together, they rolled up their blankets and set off again into the woods. Hefthon tried to tell himself that Gath Odrenoch would be fine. After all, the goblins scarcely looked any more threatening than fairies now. But still a dull unease undergirded his thoughts. He knew the creative power of the fairies. If the goblins had unlocked an equal power, he shuddered to imagine what they might destroy.

* * *

Wagon wheels creaked in the darkness around Gath Odrenoch. A long stream of carts and pedestrians jostled their way through the gatehouse, horses whinnying and children mewling in their mothers' arms. Inside, a group of deputies assigned sleeping quarters and issued commands regarding food distribution. The blacksmith stood beside a table of his wares, welcoming the frightened farmers to purchase their sense of security.

Geuel stood in the watchtower at the wall's southeastern corner. Behind him, in the center of the tower, the fortress's flagpole scraped at the night sky, its pale pennant rippling in the wet wind. A new broadsword hung at Geuel's side, a plain piece unadorned and slightly loose in the handle. Around the wall, his fellow guards stood silent and watched the stir of nothing through night's shadows. Beside Geuel, Toman leant on the haft of his spear, an oversized iron helmet drooping over his right brow.

"You can get some sleep, you know," Toman said. "You're not actually on duty."

Geuel nodded. "Maybe later. I just want to watch for now. At least until everyone's inside."

"So, did you kill any?" Toman asked.

Geuel glanced over puzzled and then realized what he meant. "Oh, yes, I suppose I killed several."

Toman's eyes glittered in the dark. "They'll worship you in the barracks tomorrow. No one's killed a goblin since the founding."

"I suppose," Geuel said.

"Tell me about the fight. What was it like when you found them in the city?"

"I don't really remember the fighting too well," Geuel replied. "It'll probably come back after I think about it. I know I killed two at least. All I remember clearly is a leg. There was a little fairy leg lying on the stairs. It was so— clean, so whole looking."

"Oh," Toman replied.

Geuel shuddered. "I don't know why I keep thinking about it."

They were silent after that, and eventually Geuel lay down in the back of the tower to sleep. He awoke to Toman shaking his shoulder.

"Geuel, Geuel!" he said, "you have to see this."

Geuel stood and looked to the south. Hundreds of dull orange lights filled the sky, like dying embers from a distant fire. The passing breeze tasted of smoke.

"Are they fairies?" Toman asked. "They must be fairies."

Geuel narrowed his eyes. He wanted to agree, to smile and rejoice that the fairies were once more flying the night skies; but he couldn't. There was something wrong about the light, something off. Not only was it dimmer but it seemed also somehow fouled, malicious. "No—no," he said slowly, "I don't think those are fairies. Toman, sound the alarm."

"They're fairies," Toman said laughing. "What else flies that way?"

Geuel ripped away the sentry horn that hung on Toman's belt and blew three short, sharp blasts. Instantly, the fort came alive with shouting soldiers and running feet. Women cried for their children and dragged them into whatever shelter they could find as the guards came rushing from their barracks in full force, mail shining in the dim starlight and faces set with the confused courage of men who have never seen war.

Soon the walls were lined with a hundred soldiers. Groups of farmers and laborers armed with an assortment of weapons and tools crowded in the fort's main square. Hounds in their kennels howled at the excitement, anxious to enter the coming fray.

Kezeik came beside Geuel and laid his hand on the younger man's shoulder. "What are they, boy?" he asked. "Do you know?"

"No, but they're not fairies."

Kezeik turned to the men on the wall. "Archers! Prepare for a volley!"

Geuel's dreams came rushing back: Gath Odrenoch burning, the blacksmith's son alone in the gate, Deni dying, his face frozen in a strange half-smile. He cast a silent prayer to Curiosity and braced himself for the coming destruction.

* * *

An eerie silence reigned in the goblin city, broken only by the scattered splashes of water from Reheuel's clothing and the distant echoes of droplets from the stalactites above. "I don't like this," Reheuel whispered as he crept through a narrow alley. "It's too quiet."

"Would you prefer opposition?"

Reheuel ignored the question and then asked, "How much farther?"

Ariel flew upward over the surrounding buildings and came back down. "Not far, maybe two hundred yards."

Reheuel slipped an arrow back onto his bowstring. "At the very least they must have left guards with the tear," he said.

They emerged then onto a wider road and Reheuel saw the tower which they were approaching. It rose nearly fifteen stories, a surprisingly slender building, terminating in a flat, bowl-shaped structure. A stone chalice fit for Faeja Himself. A heavy oak door opened onto the street where Reheuel walked.

The windows on each side of the street were still and silent, but still Reheuel felt watched as he approached the tower. He walked with a perpetual flinch, ready to turn and fire in an instant. When he reached the base of the tower, he paused to admire its construction. The entire surface was indeed one stone, but it was carved all around in murals and reliefs of old battles. Men and elves stood side by side, the men resplendent in their gilt armor, the elves wild and fierce in their leathers and tattoos. And, pressing them back, always locked in combat but with a slight upper hand, were the minotaurs. Great, hulking beasts with hooves as large as a man's head, they bellowed and tore their way across the mural, obviously idealized by the artist but still representing an unimaginable ferocity.

"The artwork is so intricate," Reheuel said in awe.

Just then a shriek rang from high above and a rock about the size of a man's fist crashed into the cobblestones near his feet. He flipped his bow upward and fired instinctively. The arrow clattered harmlessly off the sill of a sixth-floor window, driving a goblin back into the tower.

Reheuel dragged heavily on the door of the tower and felt it slowly give. His arms bulged and strained at the exertion, and he wondered briefly how many goblins it must take to open this same door. A shaft whistled down over his shoulder as he stepped out farther from the wall. He ducked quickly in through the door and drew another arrow.

Shrieks rang throughout the tower's stone passages, dozens of high pitched nickerings followed by the scrabble of clawed feet on stone. Reheuel found himself in a kind of wide entryway, three passages leading off into the tower. At the end of one he could see a staircase.

"Through there," Ariel called. "It's near the top."

Reheuel ran forward several steps and then heard the skittering of claws in the hallway behind him. He spun around and let an arrow fly, striking an oncoming goblin in the chest. Its sickle-shaped sword fell to the floor as it went down writhing. He jumped the stairs six at a time, often nearly falling as his booted feet struggled for a grip on the narrow ledges. Ariel flew along at his side, her light burning brightly with excitement.

As they climbed higher, the sounds of their enemies flooded the tower around them. Claws skittered on the stairs below and doors slammed in the distance. Snarls and yowls echoed through the hallways. Halfway up the spiral staircase, Reheuel stopped with his back to a closed pinewood door. He braced himself there and drew his sword. "Watch above," he said to Ariel.

Seconds later, a mass of long slender limbs shot around the bend of the stair and the bodies of four goblins dragged themselves into view. Reheuel swung downward once and ground his blade along the edge of a stair. Rock powder and shards spattered into the goblins' faces where they hung near the floor.

The group of them recoiled quickly, scrabbling over one another back against the wall. One overbalanced and fell screaming down the stairs. Reheuel lunged forward quickly and caught another across the shoulder, neatly severing its trapezius. The remaining two screeched and ducked down low, sweeping out their sickled blades at Reheuel's ankles.

He backed up the stairs slowly, swinging his sword but struggling to reach them. Their long, snaking bodies clung to the steps far below him as their sickles sought for his ankles. He stumbled twice on the narrow steps, and then one of their sickles caught his boot. The rusted blade barely bit into the thick leather, but the force still dragged Reheuel off his feet. He crashed heavily to his back and dropped his sword. It clattered uselessly down the stairs. He felt his bow snap beneath him.

In a moment, the goblins were on him, struggling to reach his vulnerable throat past his heavy cloak. He put up his arms and batted at them, knocking aside their reaching arms and blades. Twice the flesh on his arms tore on their swords, but his heavy sleeves took the brunt of the damage. Finally, his grasping right hand took hold of one of their throats. He swung its body across his chest and knocked the other goblin into the wall. They snarled and spat, the one he held biting deeply into his wrist. He kicked out at the other one with his boot and sent it flying down the stairs into the round wall. With one hand freed, he slid his dagger out of his belt and plunged it into the goblin he held, pumping the handle until the writhing ceased.

He struggled to his feet then and saw the three living goblins on the stairs, two bleeding and the other favoring its left arm. He lifted a sickle-sword from the stairs next to him and threw it, a short, half-rotation throw. The curved blade sunk into the farthest goblin's chest, and it dropped down the stairwell.

He tossed his dagger back to his right hand and crouched over the stairs, waiting for another attack. The remaining goblins, however, turned and scurried back down the stairs, their frustrated chunnering fading with their footsteps.

Reheuel sheathed his dagger and turned back to Ariel. "Maybe some help next time?" he said as they started climbing.

Ariel shrugged. "You didn't need it yet."

As they neared the final floor, Reheuel heard the sound of claws once more on the stairs below him. A large, studded oak door stood closed at the end of the stairs. Reheuel grabbed the iron ring set in its edge and dragged it open. Passing the door, he found himself in the cup of the tower's chalice, a massive room with bowled walls and a ceiling of latticed stone and transparent diamond wood panes.

The first thing he saw was the Tear, a stunning white gem the size of a plum—it lay on a kind of altar carved up from the floor in the room's center. The second thing he saw was the minotaur. It stood at the far end of the room, nearly seven feet tall and breathing in long, snorting drags. Heavy strands of mucus ran from its dark, bovine nose, and its matted black fur hung in ragged dreadlocks over its human shoulders. Its hooves were cracked and infected, jagged from constant wear. Pussy bubbles and sores stood out on its mangy shanks.

Chapter 10

The night sky roiled in deep shades of black and purple, heavy clouds blotting out the light of the celestial bodies. But still the wall glowed and flickered with the gyrating shadows of the sentries as the cloud of ember lights grew nearer. Geuel slid his fingers gently along the string of his new bow, feeling the beeswax spread over his fingertips. An arrow hung listlessly on his undrawn string, and six more protruded from a bag of hay before him.

Kezeik stood at the corner of the tower, his face glowing in the light of a nearby brazier. His wrinkled forehead glistened with pooling sweat, and several tendrils wound down past the crow's feet near his eyes. He looked very old in that moment, more run down than the ancient hound whose head rested against his thigh.

The approaching cloud was clearer now, a field of single lights rather than a mere glow. Kezeik nodded to Geuel and Toman. "Ready, lads?"

Geuel nodded silently, and Toman grinned.

"Consider this your induction," Kezeik said with a kindly smile. "As of now you're both members of the guard."

He turned back to the wall on their left. "Archers! Ready!" Fifty strings slid back to fifty cheeks, and fifty arms lifted their bows in a ragged salute to death. "Fire!"

The arrows hissed from the wall in a stuttering salvo, a staggered volley spaced over nearly two seconds. They glided upward from the parapet and vanished in the darkness before even reaching their peak.

"Ready! Aim! Fire!"

A second volley, slightly more uniform this time, whipped out into the night. Still the cloud of lights drew nearer, distinct now. Each light formed a slender oval of about six inches, just larger than a fairy. With each volley of arrows, the cloud undulated slightly, individual lights flickering in random directions, giving the impression of a swirling current within the cloud. But the cloud kept coming. Geuel never saw a single light disappear in the four volleys that the archers fired. They simply shifted, flickered, and returned.

Finally, when the front edges of the cloud lay a mere hundred feet out, Kezeik dropped his bow. "Shields!" he called, and the walls rang with the click of falling bows and the dull clatter of wood and leather as men fitted their shields over their vambraced arms.

Geuel squinted at the lights as they approached, striving to narrow his focus to one figure, hoping to see his enemy. They were darker than he expected, glowing only in threaded veins, like the embers of a dying fire. Their bodies were black and choked with the smoke that enveloped them and emanated from within them. Whole portions of their body were formed of smoke, thick wreaths that rippled across their limbs and torsos, disturbing the natural flesh and leaving it still whole in its wake. Their bodies and features were unmistakably goblin when visible but distorted by a smoldering inner light. They seemed exhausted by their own flames, hanging constantly on the verge of final consummation.

They passed over shrieking in a cloud, and in their wake thick billows of ashy smoke rolled across the wall, stinging the eyes of the guards and sending several men into thick coughing fits. Toman coughed twice and clawed at his eyes, trying to clear them and to stay alert. Geuel drew his coat over his nostrils and breathed in shallow drags. As the center of their cloud poised over the wall, the goblins wheeled around and descended. Shields rang and sparks flashed in the night as flaming bodies struck the sentry ranks. Shrieks both human and goblin echoed through the foothills around the city.

A tiny flash of light shot toward Geuel's chest, and he swung his shield to bat it away. The shape dissipated around the shield's edge, and Geuel swung right through it, leaving only tendrils of smoke in the wake of his blow. A throaty chuckle rippled from the smoke as it weaved back into its original form. A tiny goblin with ragged crow-like wings flashed from the smoke toward Geuel's face. He staggered backwards, swinging his sword twice and both times watching the goblin easily slip around its edge.

A column of smoke sprouted in the goblin's hand and consolidated into a vicious stiletto. It flew forward and thrust. Geuel swung his gloved hand and batted the creature off balance. It flashed downward and buried the stiletto in Geuel's thigh, instantly dissipating back to smoke. Around the wall, men cried out in shock and fear as their blades carved harmless gaps in wreathes of smoke, as intangible blades formed and cut before their very eyes. Tiny hands sprouting from tendrils of ash grasped and clawed at patches of exposed skin. Tiny arrows of ember embedded into sentries' eyes.

A cry to Geuel's right tore his attention away from his own wound as he struggled to tie a bandage into place. Toman was rising into the air, rings of smoke circled tightly around his wrists, his ankles bound by a shadowy, glowing form. His wrists smoked with the heat of pressing coals, and his eyes flashed from side to side in terror. Geuel grabbed him by the leg and struggled to pull him down, slashing carefully at the smoke around his ankle. As his blade hit the smoke, it faded to nothing and Toman's legs swung free. The bands around his wrists faded off and formed into two goblins in the air nearby. Toman fell heavily to the tower floor, his body jolting on the wooden planks.

Geuel heard then the spit of burning pine, the crackle of sap boiling in flame. The walls around the city burned, lighting the entire courtyard in a freakish network of shifting glows. Lights like embers flashed in clouds and solitary arcs all through the city, spinning into smoke and emerging in fire to strike, shrieking and cackling in voices fully goblin and yet equally something more.

Geuel and Toman stood nearly back-to-back in the tower's center, separated only by the stout flagpole of the Iris, batting with their shields at the tendrils of smoke that swerved toward them like the tentacles of some central beast. Nearly every time the smoke merely dissipated, but once Geuel was rewarded by the meaty thud of flesh against his shield and the weight of a body ricocheting back into the shadows. Kezeik was nowhere to be seen, having moved down to the nearby wall where the fighting was heaviest. Geuel could still hear his voice shouting orders from the fray, orders not meant to be heeded but merely shouted to remind those fighting that command still reigned in the battle.

Geuel heard a sharp cry behind him followed by the fade of a departing cackle. "Took one in the shoulder," Toman said, "don't know how much longer I can keep this up."

Geuel swung his shield hard and felt the reverberations rattle his arm as it swept through a cloud of smoke and struck the tower wall. "We can't leave," he said. "We have to hold the standard."

Toman grunted as he swung at a passing streak. "I'm not dying for a shred of silk. Let's get to the others."

He staggered toward the stairs leading to the courtyard, and Geuel circled the flagpole uneasily, struggling not to leave his back exposed. He glanced at the wall over the gate. It was deserted now, nearly engulfed in flames and littered with the bodies of its guards. Around the city, the other walls were mostly bare. Groups of two or three stood here and there along their expanse, back-to-back as Geuel and Toman had been. The remaining soldiers were in the courtyard, milling in tight groups behind their shields. Several soldiers had shed their weapons and were throwing water on the walls of the burning granary. Unarmed, they didn't last long.

A sharp, sudden pain filled Geuel's left side as he felt a burning dagger enter below his lowest rib. He collapsed to his knees and swung his sword behind him, feeling his hand pass through a cloud of fading smoke.

Screams came from above as well as below now. As the goblins adjusted to their new form, they discovered various advantages to flight. Soldiers caught alone were dragged high into the air over Gath Odrenoch and dropped back on their own comrades like trebuchet shot.

Geuel staggered to his feet and swung at a passing tendril of smoke as it moved toward the outer wall. He felt his shield strike something solid and a spatter of blood sprayed his face. He closed his eyes to shield them from the spray, and when he opened them again, he faced over the outer wall toward the south. The trees glowed with a new light in the distance, a bright shimmer of sunlight. It was surely too early for dawn, but still that golden light glistened on the emerald trees. And then he saw them. A cloud of new lights, purer and cleaner than the lights of the goblins. Lights as fresh as daybreak.

Geuel turned back from the wall and looked over the town. The whole of its southern sector was ablaze now. Flames licked at the stairs of the very tower where he stood. The hospital still lay several streets out of reach of the flames, but even the youngest child huddled beneath the beds of the wounded could feel its city falling. Many of the women and children, some younger than twelve, had poured out into the main courtyard. In their hands were a variety of weapons: cleavers and mallets and clubs fashioned from chair legs. And still the goblins swirled and writhed through the streets in columns of smoke, seeking out the weaker targets, the small and the isolated.

A flash of smoke shot upward to Geuel's tower, and he prepared to swing his shield; but the goblin ignored Geuel and landed on top of the pole, using its hands to burn through the ropes holding the flag. Geuel tore off his shield and hurled it like a discus, splitting the creature in half where it crouched. He watched his shield strike the earth of the courtyard and drew out his sword and dagger. He knew the end was coming.

* * *

The minotaur's eyes rolled in its skull as it drew in a deep breath through its crusted nostrils. Its body quivered with anticipation at Reheuel's scent, but it remained still. Clutching his dagger in his hand, Reheuel took a few steps forward. The creature's eyes slid after him, reddened with burst blood vessels. Its scarred chest heaved with its ragged breathing, but it remained still. Reheuel approached until he stood beside the altar, and still the beast hung back, just watching. That was when Reheuel noticed the collar, a heavy iron ring bolted around its neck. A thick chain ran out through a slit in the wall to an adjoining room. Reheuel lifted the Tear and began backing up. Just then he heard the sound of a slamming bolt from the door behind him.

A howl of laughter broke from the next room, and the chain on the minotaur's neck slackened. It took a tentative step forward.

"Reheuel," Ariel said, tensing and sliding her tiny dagger from its sheath.

"I know," he replied.

Then it was charging. It lowered its head like a true bull and shot forward, snorting in animal rage. Reheuel dove to the side and listened to the shuddering crunch as the beast's skull struck the wall. A few shards of rock fell onto his cerulean cloak as he struggled to stand back up. The creature wheeled on him, its eyes wide now with adrenaline. It lifted the chain that hung from its neck and began to twirl it over its head. Reheuel moved toward the center of the room, struggling to stay out of the range of its weighted flail.

Ariel circled it above, flashing and shifting the intensity of her light to distract it, to give Reheuel some chance of attack.

Reheuel circled the altar in the center of the room, keeping it between himself and the swirling chain. As he moved, his thoughts ran in circles, struggling to comprehend what he was seeing. The minotaurs were gone, finished. An ancient story to tell rebellious children.

He ducked as the chain lashed out over his head.

A story that could take your head off.

He glanced to the creature's chain and collar, to the sores that covered its body. It was clearly some kind of slave, perhaps barely sentient, some straggling descendant of a domesticated breed. He almost felt saddened, seeing a member of such an ancient race reduced to the state of an animal.

The chain shot out once more, low this time, and struck the base of the altar. It wrapped twice and lodged there. As the minotaur dragged at it, Reheuel ran its length and slashed at the back of the minotaur's leg, hoping to sever a tendon. The blade went high and merely nipped the muscles of its thigh. It bellowed and swung out its arm, catching his shoulder and sending him flying against the wall. He slumped to the ground, and the Tear tumbled from his hand.

Ariel flew to his shoulder and struggled to drag him upright. "We have to get out," she said breathlessly. "It's too strong."

He shook himself to clear his head and stop the world from spinning. "Get a door open," he said, "I'll keep it busy."

He ran toward the minotaur again on its other side and slashed for its leg. This time it kicked backwards and sent its hoof past his face, barely missing him as he rolled to the side and circled back in front.

Ariel flew to the door where the minotaur had been chained and found a large keyhole below its cast-iron knob. She slid her arm inside and slowly filled the keyhole with her solid light, gently levering the tumblers into position. The lock gave with a rusty click, and she pulled back from the door.

Just then a sound like brittle thunder exploded behind her. She spun to see the altar torn off its base. The chain of the minotaur shot away from it, and the creature turned again on Reheuel, ignoring the chain this time and advancing with its meaty hands opened wide. Reheuel backed up against the far door and waited for a chance to strike.

Ariel saw the distance close. Ten feet, five. Then she shot forward and extended her arm. A shield of pure light materialized in Reheuel's hand, and he lifted it in front of him, catching the first of a salvo of blows. The minotaur's fists bloodied and tore on the shield as it beat madly, and Reheuel edged out into the open.

Reheuel thrust out once with his dagger, but the tiny blade barely did more than nick the beast's hand and anger it further. Ariel floated near the ceiling and held out her arm stiffly, trembling with the exertion, her body rebelling at the abuse of its power. She could feel her link to Innocence fading as she maintained an instrument of warfare.

Reheuel held his own now, backing up constantly under the barrage of blows but blocking successfully and occasionally lashing out with his shield. But he was tiring. His movements were reserved and careful. Soon he would weaken. Ariel lifted her other arm and clenched her fists, drawing out a sword blade of light from his small dagger. She screamed in pain as she felt her ties to Innocence splinter. Barely a thread still held Ariel to her power.

Reheuel lashed out with the sword and caught the minotaur on the arm. It bellowed and ran forward, striking his shield and bowling him over onto his back. The shield shattered and faded to dust as Ariel lost her hold on it. Reheuel drew the sword to his chest and held it up as the minotaur collapsed on top of him, its massive hands closing on his head.

The web of meat beneath its thumbs covered his eyes, but he still felt the slide of his blade as it penetrated the beast's chest. Its fingers loosened from his head, and he felt its three-hundred-pound body slide to the floor. Reheuel went to pull the sword from its chest but found only his dagger, buried in an oversized wound.

Ariel knelt on the floor nearby, her light flickering dim and weak, her eyes glassy. The shock of gray in her hair, almost gone since the day before, had come back fully now. She looked old. Reheuel lifted her and the Tear from the floor and placed them both in his pack. Then he went to the unlocked door and slid it open. A goblin, seeing him come out and the dead beast behind him, shrieked in terror and scurried away down the stairs. Reheuel followed, muscles tensed and his dagger clutched at the ready.

* * *

Geuel swung his sword, felt the rush of air as it harmlessly carved through a swath of smoke, and then crumpled as a blade pierced his stomach. He dropped his dagger and groped at the area in front of his wound; but the goblin had already dissipated. He saw two more rising toward the tower and lifted his sword. As he prepared to swing, his shadow in front of him suddenly sharpened and a blast of light flooded the courtyard below. The air rushed around him, and he felt the rustle of silk clothing brush his hair as hundreds of tiny bodies flooded over the wall of the city. Bright, silvery voices rang in high-pitched war cries, inflected with a savagery wholly alien to their beauty.

The two goblins turned to flee and were impaled with a volley of tiny gleaming javelins. The javelins faded away as the goblins plummeted to earth, the embers in their bodies turning to ash. Geuel laughed out loud as the fairies rushed past him, score upon score. Their gleaming little figures burned with excitement and lit the whole courtyard with the light of day.

The goblins shot upward to meet their new enemies in the air, striving to escape the reach of human weapons. The fairies followed, lights striking lights in the air, twinkling and fading and then gleaming like gnomish fireworks. The smoke offered no protection against the fairy weapons, and the goblins reeled at first beneath their onslaught. Ember-filled bodies rained from the sky to spatter on the cobblestones and roofs of Gath Odrenoch.

After the goblins had recovered their bearings though, they quickly turned the tide. Geuel watched as the lights of both armies scattered across the sky in spirals supernaturally fast and tight. Tiny javelins flickered like lightning bolts from the hands of the fairies. But the goblins dodged and wreathed around those flickered lights. And whenever an ember glow neared a circle of sunlight, the sunlight faded and fell.

The battle looked like two colliding meteor showers, dozens of arcing lights intermingling until two struck and one dissolved. Tiny bodies peppered the earth like raindrops in a slow drizzle. Gradually, the fairies began to weaken, and many flew down to the level of the city, trying to draw their enemies in close to the human soldiers. The last light Geuel saw lower was a blazing green one, brighter than all the rest.

As the fairies lowered, the men opened their ranks to shield them, giving them momentary respite from the battle. The goblins remained poised in the sky, flickering up and down with indecision. Geuel watched the green light approach his tower and smiled to see Randiriel. "You came!" he cried.

Randiriel landed on the wall of the tower and finished tying a bandage around her bleeding arm. "So, this is the Iris on sky-blue silk," she said, nodding to the standard.

"More beautiful for her scars," Geuel replied, glancing momentarily at the charred cloth above them, shot through with burns and tears.

"Then let us bleed for her," Randiriel said, clenching her fist and forming a silver sword.

The goblins descended.

Geuel dropped his sword and tore the small brazier from its mooring, wielding it like a flaming club. Randiriel flew behind him, and they braced themselves for the battle. She felt the air stir from the rippling standard above her, and she thought of all the men who must have stood beneath this very symbol, struggling for their survival. She thought of men weary and hungry stooped beneath it in camps of defeat, of victors proudly unfurling it from the flagpoles of cities newly won. She thought of it hanging over the seats of judges and kings, its presence an eternal reminder that law reigned over men. She felt the blood running from her arm, and she felt a part of something greater than herself, of a tradition and a heritage.

A blade raced toward her, extended from a cloud of smoke, and she knocked it aside with her sword. A goblin shrieked in the smoke and veered off to the left. She lifted her sword like a javelin, and as she lifted it, it molded into one. She cast it and watched a goblin spiral out of the air, pierced through the chest. A new sword formed in her hand.

Three goblins came flying at Geuel, their ember bodies gleaming intensely from within their clouds of smoke. He swung his brazier wide and felt it lighten as its coals flung out into the air. One goblin flopped to the ground, struck by a burning coal, and Randiriel flashed down to finish it off. The other two dissipated and flowed past Geuel, forming again behind him.

He spun around in time to receive two spears buried in his chest. He felt the spearheads broadening slowly beneath his skin, widening the small wounds and burrowing deeper into his chest. He tore one out with his right hand and grasped at the spear's owner, feeling only smoke writhe away between his fingers. He sank to his knees as the other spear still grew, as large as a true dagger now. A flash of green streaked in front of him and Randiriel slammed into the remaining goblin, burying her sword to its hilt.

Geuel gasped as the spear inside his chest changed to smoke and blood flowed onto his cloak. He rolled backward onto the floor of the tower and turned a hazy gaze to the sky. Above him the Iris still waved in the glow of the burning buildings. Smoke billowed from the walls, drifting north over the city. Randiriel hovered beside the flagpole, parrying the thrust of a goblin.

Blackness robbed Geuel of any further sight.

* * *

Skittering claws echoed in the keep of the goblin city. Reheuel's heavy boots crunched on the edges of the tiny stairs as he hurried down toward the streets. Occasionally he heard the growling yips of goblins behind the doors he passed, but he barely slowed, knowing that escape was his best chance for survival.

Many times in his descent, he nearly fell, his boots snapping off a corner of a stair or slipping on a patch of worn stone; but he kept his balance and, after an eternity of dreamlike circling down the winding stairs, he reached the street. He ran quickly down the alleys he had come by, splashing through the tiny rivulets of water that ran toward the nearby river. Several arrows spat shards of stone about his ankles as they skipped off the cobbled streets, and the sound of twanging bowstrings echoed from the heights of the sealed city. Reheuel tried to ignore the sounds and kept running, his heart thumping wildly in his chest and his lungs swelling to refresh his failing muscles.

By the time he reached the river, he had lost track of his pursuers. He entered the shallow water at a run and tumbled into his canoe, tossing his backpack into the prow. A sharp cry sounded from inside as it rolled into place. He lifted his punting pole and slammed it down into the water, sending the craft downriver in a rapid but awkward glide. An arrow buried itself in the side of the canoe, and he continued punting, his eyes fixed on a distant exit in the wall of the city-cavern.

Twice more as he rode, arrows sang past him; but they clattered harmlessly off far-off walls, wild shots taken from a distance. As he neared the exit, his backpack opened and Ariel crept out, her light still dim but with a quality more perfect and pure than Reheuel had seen since the Tear was first taken. The Tear within the bag glowed with an equal perfection, sending out tiny flashes of sunlight through the wrinkles of the backpack's opening.

Just then Reheuel saw shapes slithering across the shadows of a building near the exit. Two goblins were creeping into position on top of the roof. Almost immediately after noting them, he saw others, dozens of them, crouching in the alleys and windows around the exit. They were cutting him off.

Ariel slid the Tear from the bag, clutching it in both hands, and lifted it over her head, dwarfed by its translucent orb. It brightened slowly at first, seeming to swell and bulge as the light in its droplet center seeped out to fill the crystal shell. Then the light broke the surface of the gem and flared outward like the rays of a tiny sun, blasting the walls and buildings in a deep and heavy glow. Reheuel covered his eyes and turned away, blinded. Even as he did so, he could feel the light intensifying, singing his clothing and burrowing through his eyelids.

The goblins shrieked, and bowstrings twanged wildly as the creatures scrabbled away from the blaze, their nocturnal eyes scarred and overloaded. The canoe passed into the cave exit unchallenged, and Ariel lowered the gem, letting its glow fade to the light of a summer day.

They drifted peacefully through the narrow tunnel, unchallenged and bathed in daylight. Reheuel uncovered his eyes and wiped away a few involuntary tears, his vision still hazy. "We made it," he said with a relieved chuckle. "They won't follow us in the light."

"You have done well," Ariel said. "You have my thanks."

"So, what now?" he asked, "will you rebuild the city?"

"If any remain to dwell there. You saw the lights bound for Gath Odrenoch."

"We'll know when we get there."

They were both silent for a while, and then Ariel pointed to the carvings that covered the cave walls. "This city is old," she said, "older than the goblins and the Iris. Perhaps older than Elicathaliss. No goblin carved these walls."

Reheuel nodded. "Minotaurs most likely. Been centuries since man had any dealings with the brutes. No telling how long that one has been chained down here."

Ariel stood on the edge of the canoe and ran her fingers over a carving of a river nymph as they passed. "They were a noble people," she said. "Their lives were counted in centuries rather than decades, and the world was a marvelous place under their rule, full of splendors forgotten by song. Their temples stood on pillars of diamond wood with minarets of steel and altars carved from living stone."

"You were there with the minotaurs?" Reheuel asked, forgetting, as he often did, just how old his companion truly was.

She nodded. "From their rise to their fall. They had a dream while they ruled. They called it *Elkinaugh*: an eternal kingdom passed down through their lineage, to last till the sun burnt out and Time unfurled the final second of its strand. But here they are, slobbering beasts chained in the caves of an inferior race. They, whose cities were the wonders of the world."

"No wonder lasts forever," Reheuel said softly, driving his pole deep into the murk beneath their craft.

"I thought my city would last for eternity," Ariel said. "But why should it last when *Elkinaugh* fades? Why should I cling to youth's innocence if it is only going to shatter?"

"Perhaps because passing beauties still bless passing lives," Reheuel replied.

The light reflecting from the carvings dimmed then as the walls ahead of the canoe gave way to the great cavern through which they had entered the goblin city. Reheuel dropped the pole into the water and lifted his dagger.

Ariel grasped the tear, and it slowly brightened, the circle of its light racing across the cavern floor to meet the flow of sunlight filtering over the outer gates. The cavern was empty aside from the small flotilla of canoes still bumping against the bridge. Reheuel sheathed his dagger, leapt ashore, and ran for the nearest stair, letting himself out over the rough wooden wall.

It was a warm morning outside, muggy with the mist of the previous day's downpour; but the fresh air still provided a welcome change from the stale cold of the caves. He felt each breath fill his body with new strength as he strode from the gates. It would take him two more days to reach Gath Odrenoch, but as he felt then, the prospect seemed a mere stroll.

Chapter 11

Hefthon sat late into the night, resting on a hilltop near the edge of the Blue Hills. Despite Tressa's desire to keep moving, they had eventually stopped to sleep. But Hefthon stayed up, watching the horizon. Far off to the north, the sky glowed orange. A thick pillar of smoke, a darker shade of night's black, grew from the center of the glow, drawing the firelight back into the surrounding darkness. Hefthon gripped his sword hilt tightly and trembled with the ache of inaction. Twice now he had been cut off from the battle and left to guard against phantom fears while others faced true danger. Gath Odrenoch burned, and he lay safe and secure in a bed of bluebarrels.

No doubt his brother was there—Toman, and Kezeik, and Deni. They were all there doing their duty. And here was Hefthon, left to the defense of those farthest removed from danger. He imagined those who were dying in the city, his friends and their families burning and bleeding. He wished in that moment that he could take all their pain on himself, that he could suffer so deeply and violently that all of those in Gath Odrenoch could be spared their share of fate's chastisement. He wished that he could be there to aid them, to protect his city. A sob crept upward from his breast, and he choked as he stifled it.

He clenched his fists before him and bowed his forehead to the ground, praying to Curiosity to protect his family and his city, begging for forgiveness for his absence. His body shuddered silently with grief and bottled energy. He wanted to run, to smash, to scream, to tear something apart and trample it into the earth. He should have been there, should have gone with Geuel to where he was needed.

The orange glow in the distance caught his eye once more as he lay there, drawing him upright. He knew that one more man would likely make little difference in the battle that raged beneath that glow, but knowledge hardly lessened his need to make what small difference he could.

He thought back to his promise to Ariel. He had known what it meant when he made it. The sacrifice of all chance at glory or fame. His life would be a mere pretense of soldiery, the guarding of a city that had gone for centuries unmolested. But he loved the Fairy City, loved it more than all the wonders of his own people combined. It was a place of purity and innocence untainted by time. And the sight of the fairies bleeding, of innocence shattered, had struck him so deeply that the loss of his own dreams seemed a mere pittance in exchange for its protection. He had meant his promise. But as he watched Gath Odrenoch burn, he wondered whether he could live with it.

He turned away from the glow in the north and ended his prayer, looking back to Tressa and Veil. They slept about ten yards off, curled in their wool blankets beneath a solitary white pine. They looked so peaceful in sleep, worlds apart from the warfare and flames in the north.

He remembered then the reason he had wanted so desperately to protect the Fairy City. Even after a thousand years of safety, it had taken just one day for the city to burn. Just one day for all of that peace to be shattered. Any moment that the innocent went unprotected was an opportunity for their suffering. And even if he spent his entire life and only raised his sword once, that one moment would be worth a life spent waiting.

Perhaps, in guarding his family, he had missed his chance for glory and action. Perhaps he would never raise his sword in their defense. But even still, if there was any chance of his presence securing their safety, did that not justify his defense?

He returned to the shelter of the pine and lay down to sleep, his face turned to the north. His eyes finally closed with the glow of Gath Odrenoch haunting his sight.

Tressa was the first to wake in the morning. She rolled up her blanket and pulled some roasted partridge from her pack, dividing it into portions for the morning meal. As she gathered the canteens, she caught sight of smoke in the distance. Thinner than it had been when Hefthon watched it in the night but still a discernible streamer, tickling the belly of the dawn sky.

She sighed and cast up a prayer for her husband and son. She had been a mere girl the first time Gath Odrenoch burned, younger than Veil. But still the sight of the smoke brought back dark memories: the scent of charred wood overhead as she cowered beneath the floorboards of her family's kitchen. Her mother had dragged her into their tiny pantry and slammed the trapdoor above them, clamping her hand tightly over her daughter's mouth.

Tressa could almost taste her mother's sweat again as she remembered a palm pressed between her lips. She could almost hear her mother's frantic, whispered assurances, meant to drown out the screams from outside and the wild laughter of the goblins.

Hefthon sat up and trudged over to her, squatting down to take his meal. "Saw the smoke?" he asked.

Tressa nodded. "Brings back memories."

"Started just after midnight.

Veil sat up then and raked her matted hair out of her eyes. "What started?" she asked.

Hefthon pointed to the north. "Fire," he said.

"Is that—home?" Veil asked, her eyes moistening.

Tressa nodded. "Save your tears, Veil. We need to travel."

They set out half an hour later, enjoying the clear, lawn-like fields of the Blue Hills after their long trudge through forests and field grass. They made decent time that day and stopped about a third of the way across. The next morning, they set out once more and made it about three quarters of the way across. The next day would bring them out of the Blue Hills, past the spot where Hefthon and Veil had sought a glimpse of the Fairy City mere weeks before. The Hills were high here, and even Gath Odrenoch in the Gath foothills lay below them. It was still hidden though, shielded behind miles of hills and forest. They filled their canteens in a narrow stream between two of the hills and made camp beside its banks. Hefthon slept fitfully, all too aware that Gath Odrenoch lay a mere two days further north.

* * *

Like fire on an open wound. That's how it felt at first. The realization came hazily, a detached recognition of pain. And then the pain morphed. It was narrower now, sharp like the sting of a needle . . . actually . . . exactly like the sting of a needle.

"Ouch!" Geuel awoke with a start, sitting up and striking his head on the bunk above him. He grunted and fell back onto the mattress, feeling a sharp tug in the flesh of his chest as he did so. He glanced down and saw, hazily, a needle and thread growing out of his ribs. He blinked a few times and let his eyes adjust. The needle was moving again by the time he could see properly, descending to enter his chest. It was held by Toman's sister, and a bottle of alcohol lay on a table beside the bunk.

He held still as she finished sewing and gradually took in his surroundings. He was in the barracks. He could tell that by the tattered flag hanging on the far wall. The room seemed brighter though than he remembered. It took him several seconds to realize why. A massive section of the roof in the southeast corner had collapsed, burned in the previous night's battle.

After Toman's sister had tied off her stitches, Geuel pulled his shoulders against the headrest and sat up a little. "What happened, Mara?" he asked, "last night? How'd it end?"

"The goblins broke shortly after the fairies arrived," Mara replied. "They scattered."

"And Toman?" Geuel asked. "I lost him during the battle. And Kezeik and Deni?"

"Toman's fine," she said, stifling a grin. "He was wounded twice, but he couldn't be happier. Tells the story to anyone who'll listen. Deni's fine too. He sent father out to find your family."

Geuel chuckled. "I'm sure Toman will be stepping high for a while now. But—what about Kezeik?"

Mara shook her head. "They found his body this morning. That old dog brought them with its howls." She choked up slightly. "The Smoke Fairies dropped him from the air."

Geuel closed his eyes and let his head slide back into the mattress. He felt the needle enter the flesh in his arm and stayed still once more. He thought back over a thousand drills repeated under Kezeik's liquid gaze, of the rare moments when some spark of pride would show in those eyes and Geuel would feel more a man than he ever had in his life. It was as if part of Geuel's reality had just disappeared, the whole world shifting to some unfamiliar form.

"The flag?" Geuel asked quietly as Mara worked, "did the flag stay planted?"

"Yes, it's there," she replied, "Deni says they found you at its base."

"And Randiriel? Have you heard what happened to her?"

"The fairy leader?" Mara asked. "Yes, she and Deni were talking in the gatehouse last I knew."

Geuel nodded. He slid his clean arm beneath his pillow and relaxed. Before long, he drifted to sleep again, and Mara finished her work. He awoke hours later and found himself alone. Around the room the light groans of the wounded and the quiet voices of those nursing them were the only sounds. He felt little real pain, but his body ached all over. His chest especially felt deeply sore, and he could barely move his arm.

He lay still for several minutes and then saw a tiny green figure flit through the barracks door. He lifted an arm and beckoned to her. Randiriel saw him, and even at a distance, he could tell she was smiling. She flew to his bedside and rested on the edge of the table. "How do you feel?" she asked, leaning back on her palms and smiling.

"Fi—" Geuel shrugged and winced at the movement, "decent given the circumstances."

"We did it," Randiriel said. "We bled for the Iris."

"And would you bleed again?" Geuel asked.

"I would. I've never felt a reason for living like I did last night."

Geuel smiled. "I would too. There's something beautiful in that symbol." Geuel paused. "How were your losses?"

"Heavy," Randiriel replied, sobering, "seven score dead. We can't count the goblins because their bodies dissipate. But Deni believes they lost two hundred."

"I'm sorry," Geuel said. "But thank you, thank you for coming."

Randiriel smiled sadly. "It was our fight too."

"At least with all the goblins here Father may have found the Tear. You can still rebuild."

"No, *Ariel* can rebuild," Randiriel replied. "I'm done with Elicathaliss. Those who came with me will find their own places now."

"And you," Geuel asked, "where's your place?"

"I don't know. I thought that I would travel, see the world with my new eyes, learn its beauties now that I appreciate their cost. There was another fairy, Rylen. We might have traveled together. But—he's gone now. Perhaps I'll fly to the Capital and see the first Iris. I've never seen the Crystal City."

Geuel smiled. "I am bound there myself one day as a conscript. Perhaps we will meet in her streets and reminisce about tonight's battle."

Randiriel smiled. "I would welcome it, my friend."

* * *

Reheuel traveled continually for a day and night after leaving the goblin city, fearing to stop in the darkness so near their home. Ariel lit his path, and he made decent time despite exhaustion. By midnight, his eyelids hung like weights and his breathing had grown ragged. But still he moved on, supporting himself on a young poplar staff he had carved in the night.

When morning came, he slept for a few hours in a clearing of ferns and then set out once more for Gath Odrenoch, anxious to see the fate of his city. He had been in the caves when the battle ended and had not seen the dispersion of lights as the goblins fled the city, flashing out in tiny clouds to every point of the compass, leaderless and aimless. If he had, perhaps he would not have worried as deeply for his people. But the cloak of his station hung heavily on his shoulders. All he could think of was how he would survive the guilt if he had outlived his city.

Night was falling when he reached the city gates. He approached quietly through the woods, his heart sinking as he saw the charred ruins of the walls, the holes where the log beams had collapsed away altogether. But as he neared the gate, he saw a human sentry in the tower, recognizing him as the town cobbler. "Garreth!" he called, walking out onto the road. "Open the gate, man."

The old man's head jerked upright, and his spear clattered against his helmet as he came to attention. He had clearly been dozing. He looked down into the road and laughed. "Captain Reheuel! Good welcome to you, Sir! There's someone here who'll certainly be glad to see you." He ran down the gatehouse stairs then and began turning the wheel to open the gate. Reheuel could have simply stepped a few feet from the road and entered through a large section of missing wall. But somehow it seemed less dignified than to use the gate. The gate was a sign of security, a sign that man still controlled the doings in Gath Odrenoch.

After Reheuel had entered and helped Garreth close the gate, Garreth led him and Ariel to the barracks. "He's right in here, Captain," Garreth said, pointing to a nearby bunk. He tipped his helmet as he backed out. "Now I'd best be getting back to the wall."

Geuel looked up from the bed where he was sitting with a bowl of beef stew. "Father!" he cried.

Randiriel, who was sitting on the bed's headboard, looked up quickly and nodded at Ariel, unsure of what to expect.

Reheuel pulled the Tear from his pack and approached his son. "Still a brash old man?" he asked, laughing.

"Beautiful, brash old man," Geuel replied, standing and putting his arms around him. The stitches in his chest and arm strained as he did so, but he hardly cared. It was worth it to feel his father's warmth in his arms. "I'm proud, Father," he said.

Reheuel clapped his back. "And I of you. Looks like you've had quite the ordeal here. Where's your mother? And your brother and sister?"

"They're not here yet," Geuel said. "I ran ahead. It's fine though. Deni sent a rider to find them. And they have Hefthon."

Reheuel nodded. "You've done well. Tell me, how are our losses?"

"They don't have an exact number yet. Many are missing. Not all made it into the city. But it looks like a hundred and fifty people all told."

Reheuel dropped his face into his hands and sank down onto his son's bunk. "A hundred and fifty?" he asked, staring at the floor, "to goblins?"

"Not goblins exactly," Geuel replied. "The people are calling them smoke fairies. They're something new."

"Deni and Kezeik?" Reheuel asked.

"Deni's alive. He's organizing things now. Kezeik, they found him yesterday morning. He didn't make it . . . None of us would have made it if it hadn't been for the fairies."

Ariel, who had been silent until then, glanced up. "Why?" she asked.

"Your weapons worked better against them than ours," Geuel said. "Your people helped win the battle."

Ariel turned to Randiriel. "You led our people to this?" she asked.

"Only those that wished to come, those lost to youth already—like me."

Ariel placed her hand on Randiriel's shoulder. "I'm sorry, Rand," she said, "I'm sorry for what you've lost."

"I'm not," Randiriel replied.

Reheuel turned to Randiriel. "Thank you," he said, wishing that he could shake her hand or clap her on the back. "We owe you a great deal."

Geuel leant back against the headboard then and started eating again. "So, Father," he asked, "what will we do about the conscripts?"

Reheuel sighed. "The Emperor will still want them. But that can wait. Gath Odrenoch is hardly a pin prick on his map. No one will care if our conscripts come a few months late. For now, we'll rebuild."

* * *

Water splashed in the stream, and Hefthon's eyes snapped open. He slid his sword softly from its sheath and hid its gleaming blade in the bluebarrels beside him. Soft, snorting breaths sounded in the night air above the water. He could dimly make out clouds of steamy breath from several large forms that stumbled through the stream.

"Stop!" he cried, standing and lifting his sword. "Name yourself!"

"Whoa! Easy, lad!" came a chuckling warning from the darkness. "It's me, Steun."

"Steun?" Hefthon asked, sheathing his sword in relief. "What are you doing out this far?"

Toman's father slid from his horse and approached, clapping Hefthon in a warm embrace. "Looking for you three," he said with a laugh. "Geuel said you might be needing a ride back to the city."

Tressa approached from the darkness. "Steun," she said, smiling, "so good to see you. How's the city?"

"It's there," Steun replied, "a little the worse for wear but still standing. I brought horses. So just climb on up and we'll head back. Geuel'll be more than happy to see you lot safe."

"Geuel's there?" Veil asked, her eyes shining so brightly that they were visible even in the darkness.

"Oh, aye, he's there, and they'll no doubt be singing ballads of his deeds by the time we get back to join him. He saved a lot of lives with his warning."

Steun stooped by the stirrup of one of the horses and helped Veil to mount. "You all look pretty tired," he said. "Hope you can still ride though. I'd like to be back by the afternoon. Lots of work left yet."

They rode at a canter, more than halving the time that they would have spent walking but still not meeting Steun's desire. It was nearing dusk when they crested the brow of a Gath foothill and saw the city below them, its walls charred and collapsed in areas, numerous houses obliterated, and the lawn outside the walls littered with rows of sorted bodies. Tressa gasped at the sight and turned her face, memories long ago repressed flooding back to haunt her. Veil's breathing quickened, but she showed no other response.

They rode down in silence and stopped outside the open gates. Dozens of people were busy in the courtyard, clearing rubble and patching the outer wall. A line of children were working the courtyard pump, passing buckets in a chain toward the hospital and barracks. Outside the walls, people were carting away bodies to the cemetery.

Tressa dismounted and walked slowly past the rows of dead, silently noting each familiar face, guessing about those too damaged to recognize. Veil held to her hand and walked beside her, tears falling unashamedly as she saw her friends and neighbors rigid and bloated in the dust. She covered her face with her collar to mask the stench.

Hefthon began to approach the bodies but stopped, his eyes caught by something else. Near the wall, a smaller field of dead lay scattered, the glow gone from every marble body, blood staining their colorful clothing and translucent wings. Over a hundred fairies were stretched out along the wall, their tiny bodies crumpled in various attitudes of pain, their faces twisted with passions previously unfamiliar. He walked among them for a while and noted the ones he had seen before. Then he left and entered the city.

In the piled bodies, he had seen the final answer to whether he could live his life as a mere sentry. Every one of those bodies had once been beautiful—and every one of them might have stayed beautiful if protected. Beauty is always worth preserving.

Hefthon found Geuel in the barracks chatting with Toman's sister. Her eyes were filled with admiration as Geuel described his journey from the Fairy city. Hefthon leant against the wall nearby and chuckled to himself as he heard what he felt must be a rather embellished account of his brother's hardships.

Geuel heard the chuckle and turned his head sharply. "Hey! Hef!" he cried, "you made it. Are Mother and Veil here?"

Hefthon approached the bedside and clapped his brother on the back, not being particularly careful of the bandages. "Yeah, they're outside," he said. "No doubt Veil's already headed for the hospital to help out."

They embraced, and Geuel began relating the state of Gath Odrenoch, both of them sobering as the casualty numbers unfolded.

Nearby in the gatehouse, Deni, Reheuel, Ariel, and Randiriel gathered around a small table, their voices lowered despite their seclusion.

"I say we follow them," Reheuel said. "We didn't before. And we're paying for it now."

"With what?" Deni asked. "Half our soldiers are dead. The other half are wounded or exhausted."

"Deni's right," Ariel said. "I won't see any more of my people die. They came here out of duty. But they needn't seek out further fighting."

Reheuel threw his hands up. "Deni! Deni! You were there! We were all grouped around those cave mouths. All of us, bloodied and sore and tired of killing. And we let it go. We came back and said, 'let them be.' And look around you now. Death is what we've reaped. We ought to finish it this time."

Deni shook his head. "There were hardly any left last night. A few score, maybe. They're not going to attack. But if we follow them, we could still lose any number of good men. I don't want more blood on my hands."

"They won't attack now, no. But what about in ten or twenty years when our sons are in our position? Or thirty or forty when it's our grandchildren? They could attack then. And we'd be long since peacefully laid to rest, our hands washed of blood. But our children will still bleed."

Randiriel shook her head. "I'd go if we could be sure of our mission. But there are few fairies left who can fight. I don't want to watch them die for my decision. They've no stake in this."

Ariel nodded her thanks and looked back to Reheuel. "The fairies cannot help you. Our race has lost enough already. It could take five hundred years to replace the lives lost in this last week. Your family is safe, Reheuel. Take the victory you have."

"Wise words," Deni said. "Listen to her, Captain. We can't afford more losses either."

Reheuel's voice came out in an even but forced tone, "It's easy for us to call this victory. We won't be here when the creatures return. They'll be some other generation's responsibility. Do we really want to let what's happened here happen again?"

Deni shook his head. "No, but I want what happened here to be over. I want it done. I want to go home and kiss my children and tell them that they're safe."

Reheuel nodded and stood. "Then do so. Because they are safe—for now." He strode from the barracks, his tone even but his eyes furious.

Deni followed him seconds later, relieved, but nagged by a vague sense of guilt.

Ariel sat down on the table. "I thought you would side with Reheuel," she said. "You were so quick to defend Gath Odrenoch."

Randiriel shook her head. "Defending this city was our duty. Our weapon placed it in danger. But I could not ask our people to fight Reheuel's battles. If he asked, I would join him myself. But I would not bring our people to further death."

"I respect that," Ariel said with a smile. "It makes me sorry that we must part."

Randiriel laughed. "The lives of fairies are long. Perhaps our paths will cross. You're rebuilding, I assume?"

Ariel nodded. "Yes, our people still need a home, and the world still needs their innocence. I will leave shortly to return the Tear. After things have settled here, please tell Reheuel to bring his family to the City of Youth. I owe them a reward."

Randiriel nodded. "I will."

"And please, see that they come," Ariel said.

As Randiriel left, she passed Brylle entering. Ariel nodded to the silver-lit fairy. "Come, Brylle, it's time," she said.

A short while later, two bright lights, one scarlet and one silver, shot over the walls of Gath Odrenoch into the darkness, a clear crystal gem suspended between them, reflecting the light of a thousand stars.

Chapter 12

The air was crisp with the warning chill of fall when Randiriel and Reheuel's family set out for Elicathaliss. As they neared the city, Randiriel rested lazily on Veil's shoulder, jolting occasionally with the movements of the horse and rider beneath her. Around them a circle of Fairies had begun to form, spinning and dancing and laughing in the cool daylight. Their lights burned all the brighter for the cold, as if their heat came from within. They sang as they spun their circles, chanting songs of the ancient days, songs of the merpeople and of minotaurs and gnomes. And once or twice, Reheuel thought he heard his own name, as if the fairies had begun to work him into their lore.

Geuel laughed and flicked some water droplets out into the crowd of fairies, scattering them in gales of tittering laughter. "Well, near-death and trauma hardly seem to have done them any harm," he said.

Randiriel flicked her head dismissively. "They're children. They'd bounce back from anything."

Veil held out a hand to some of the nearer fairies, letting one tentatively alight on her fingertip. She opened her mouth in awe and tried to draw it closer. It shot away in a flash, laughing merrily over its shoulder. "Did you see that, Father?" Veil asked.

Reheuel nodded. "You have a gentle way, daughter," he said, "they'll trust you more easily than your brothers."

Randiriel rolled her eyes at the departing fairy. "Flighty little thing," she said. "You've got a fairy sitting on your shoulder too, you know."

"Yeah, but it's not the same," Veil said.

"Would it help if I spun a cartwheel? Or chortled like a water sprite?" Randiriel asked.

"That'll be the day," Hefthon said.

Randiriel ignored him. "At least *I've* developed some dignity," she said.

The city rose before them now, larger even than before, with crenelated, silver walls and buttressed towers capped by tear-shaped domes. Every building terminated in a slender spire, like the weening tip of a teardrop symbol. Most had squat, circular bases of varying width. Overall, the city gave the impression of a scattered field of giant tears striking a pool of water, each tear submerged to a different level. And, as before, its central square hung in a great arc over the waters of the Faeja, planted on either bank by great, silver causeways, suspended by diamond-colored cables that ran upward to a network of high arches.

In the sky over the city, great clockwork gears of solid light spun and gyrated in various fantastic designs, shifting the walls and tunnels of an ever-changing three-dimensional maze, a favorite plaything of the fairies.

Ariel stood on a pedestal at the head of a flight of steps that descended from the raised main gate. Her light was as healthy and clear as it had been on the first day she met them, and her scarlet dress shone brightly even in the midday sun. Only the shock of gray in her hair remained as a reminder of her ordeals.

"Welcome," she said, waving a hand to her guests. "Please, let my people bring your horses to the stables and follow me inside. We have a banquet prepared in the keep."

Reheuel and his family descended, and dozens of fairies flitted to the horses' bridles to lead them away, tugging softly and whistling to draw them along. Randiriel flew to Ariel's pedestal and extended her hand. "Ariel," she said.

Ariel smiled and took her hand. "Welcome, Rand. I'm glad you came."

Randiriel nodded. "Then I'm welcome?" she asked.

"As a guest and as a friend, you shall never be turned away from these gates," Ariel replied. "It is only as a citizen that you will no longer find a place."

Just then the sound of a tin whistle began within the gate. Several others answered, and Ariel turned to her guests. "They're bidding us to the table. Come, let us dine."

They entered the gates as a group, and as they moved through the streets, hundreds of whistles all around the city joined the song. They echoed off the silver walls and amplified through the tiny tunnels that threaded the buildings. After a few minutes, it was impossible to tell where any of the music was coming from. It filled the air in an even blanket, echoes trundling after faded notes. As if the city itself were lifting its voice in song.

They entered the banquet hall and a thousand petals rained down around them, rose and bluebarrel, daisy and iris. A gentle breeze sifted in through the tiny holes that ringed the walls and stirred the flowers in the air, slowing their descent. Veil laughed and caught at them as they fell. Above them, hundreds of fairies circled, scattering the petals and sometimes chasing after them nearly as fast as they dropped them.

A great stone table stood in the center of the hall with high-backed silver chairs around it. The surface was carved in shallow strokes to form a full map of Rehavan, from the southern jungles to the northern wastes and the eastern shores to the western deserts. The table was set at a height for humans, but on top of it and covering half of its oval surface, a second table rose, a great diamond-wood ring just inches tall and lined with hundreds of tiny chairs on both its inner and outer edge. Ariel waved her guests to their seats and took her own place in a chair of woven golden wire at the higher table. To her left and right, the members of the council sat down.

Reheuel led his family to the table and drew out a chair for his wife. Randiriel ignored the fairy table and sat down cross-legged on the tabletop near the humans. After a few seconds, a flood of tiny forms came winging in through numerous doors and passages in the walls. They carried trays of berries and pastries between them, tiny cakes twice the size of their own bodies, baked with wild honey and fresh cream. Steady streams of grape juice and cinnamon-laced apple cider flowed down from unseen funnels in the ceiling, trickling down runners in the walls to collect in large basins carved into the backs of grotesque statues on the walls. Tiny sluices in the statues' mouths opened to fill the diners' goblets.

Ariel sat at the head of the table and watched as the humans ate and laughed, pointing to the different mechanisms with which the fairies managed their service: the nets to carry the pastries, slung between a dozen fairies; the miniature siege towers full of peaches; and the little wheelbarrows full of jellies and butter. None of them had ever tasted cinnamon before, or peaches. The meal passed in great joy.

"Tell me, Brylle, why did you help defend Gath Odrenoch?" Ariel asked, turning away from watching her guests to the fairy beside her.

"I didn't defend Gath Odrenoch," Brylle replied. "I defended our people."

"But you were the only council member who fought. Why?"

"Because the pure ones cannot fight. I had to protect them."

Ariel pointed across their table to where the humans were eating. "Watch," she said. A troupe of fairies were braiding Veil's hair again, listening in rapt attention as she told them stories of her farm. Several others were teaching Tressa the words of a song. The lines of care and worry that had etched their way into her face since the battle were all melting away. Her eyes filled with a light unseen in months. Hefthon was kneeling beside the table and lecturing a group of fairies about the design their fruit cart. Geuel and Randiriel were discussing something more abstract to judge by their gestures, something far removed from the City of Youth. But even they sat a little more relaxed, smiled a little more readily, than they would have outside that city. Reheuel leant back in his chair, his hands folded behind his head, and simply watched as his family found a moment of bliss.

"Do you see it?" Ariel asked.

"Their happiness?" Brylle said uncertainly.

"You see the effects of innocence on this world," Ariel said. "What you see is the reason that the Fairy City exists. It is a place of respite to bless those who know toil and pain. A sight of innocence for a breaking world."

"It's beautiful," Brylle said.

"Would you die for it?" Ariel asked.

Brylle paused, surprised at the suddenness of the question. "Yes, I suppose I would," she said.

Ariel smiled sadly. "So would I," she said, "and someday I will. When that happens, I want you to take my place."

Brylle laughed. "You'll outlive us all," she said. "A thousand years ago, you were already an ancient story."

Ariel nodded. "Yes, but after today, my days are numbered. Perhaps millennia, perhaps just decades, but my hourglass is about to finally tip, to begin its run toward the end."

Brylle's smile faded. "What do you mean?"

"I used to think it beautiful how men could live in the shadow of their deaths. Today, for the first time, I will begin to understand it. Today I shed my immortality. Nothing lasts forever."

Ariel rose then before Brylle could speak and tapped her knife against her crystal goblet. Instantly, the hundreds of fairies scattered across the hall stilled themselves and grew silent. Reheuel stood and looked questioningly at Ariel.

She smiled at him. "Reheuel," she said, "you have done my people a great service, one that we could never truly repay. However, I promised Geuel that his father's courage would not go wholly unrewarded. So, today, I wish to present you with a gift, something that humanity has always desired."

She beckoned forward a group of fairies who hovered in the main doorway and flew down to the center of the table where Reheuel and his family sat. A few dozen fairies immediately cleared off the table, and the fairies in the doorway flew forward, lowering a cloth-wrapped bundle at Ariel's feet.

From the cloth, Ariel slid her Tear. It shone brilliantly in the light of the fairies gathered there, seeming to reflect each of their lights uniquely in its crystal shell. "If you would all stand still," Ariel said, "I would be grateful."

She knelt down and pressed one hand firmly on the Tear, extending the other directly toward Reheuel's chest. Her body trembled with a surge of energy, and the Tear blazed. Her arm grew translucent in the light of the Tear and then filled with its own extreme energy, turning white and then disappearing in a pillar of blinding light. Her body flashed, her head snapped backwards, and a great column of light shot from her extended hand to strike Reheuel's chest. There was no impact as it struck, just a fantastic, vibrant glow that spread through his body and then dissipated through his face and fingertips.

The hall shuddered as Ariel continued pressing down on the Tear, and the fairies quaked where they stood and floated, awed by the power they felt running out from their collective. Ariel turned her hand to Tressa next, sending out a second blinding light. Tressa glowed with yellow sunlight and sighed as if a great pain were leaving her. All remains of care fled her face with the fading of the light, and she straightened feeling five years younger.

Three more times, Ariel directed her blasts of light, once to each of Reheuel's children. And when she had finished, she slid her hand from the Tear and sank to her knees. A tiny black handprint sizzled in the surface of the Tear, a permanent scar in what was thought its unbreakable surface.

Reheuel and his family glanced at each other uncertainly, each overcome with a sudden feeling of health and vigor but unsure of what had actually happened.

Ariel smiled at them. "Recently, a great evil was released on this world, a new race born from this Tear. Today, it has granted life to a new good. Barring accidents of physical harm and injury in combat, you are each now immortal, the first family of a line that will no doubt bless this world for centuries to come."

Reheuel glanced down at his hands. Leathery and scarred with age. "Immortal?" he asked.

Ariel smiled. "As much as I have been. You will never age, never grow sick, never collapse beneath the blows of time alone."

Reheuel shook his head. "I don't know what to say."

Ariel laughed. "Then let us finish our celebration. Let us raise our glasses to coming centuries of friendship."

The rest of the afternoon passed in storytelling and song, the humans and fairies exchanging the tales each held unique to their people. The fairies sang stories of the merfolk and gnomes, and Reheuel told stories of the rugged north, of fire sprites and sand dragons and the wild men who hunt them.

In the evening, Hefthon approached the Fairy Queen where she sat alone in the courtyard. "Ariel," he said, "I made you a promise when last we spoke."

She nodded. "It was a promise made in passion. I do not hold you to it."

"I am grateful, but I would hold myself to it nonetheless."

"So, you would give your life to this city?" Ariel asked, "even knowing how long it now might be?"

Hefthon nodded. "I travel to the Capital this winter. There I will serve for four years as a soldier. But—after— when I am free again, I will return. The world needs this city. And I would be honored to help protect it."

"Then I will see you in four years," Ariel said.

The next morning, Reheuel and his family rode back toward Gath Odrenoch, and Brylle and Ariel stood on the wall over the gate waving farewell. Ariel believed that her aging would come slowly, perhaps over the span of centuries. But as they stood there together, Brylle thought that already her hair looked slightly grayer, that her light burned slightly duller. Brylle shivered in the chill of the fall wind. No wonder lasts forever.

Epilogue

The story-man's voice faded as he pronounced the final sentence of his story, his eyes taking on a distant nostalgia, as if he were pained by a thousand memories that echoed Brylle's sentiment. The tale had taken many nights, but still the size of his audience had scarcely diminished. And now, as the story ended, the people shuffled uncomfortably, hesitant to make their final departure from the fantasy they had so briefly entered.

A small child near the foot of the little stage raised his hand and called out to the story-man, "What happened to them?"

The child's mother hushed him, but still the entire crowd leaned forward, eager for any last remnant of the tale, no matter how familiar.

The story-man smiled at the child and beckoned him forward. He set the boy on his knee and continued, addressing the child personally but speaking so that all in the tent could hear him.

"Many things, child, many things happened to the people in our story. For our story was but the first chapter in the legend of The Father, a tale that would unfold for further centuries in Reheuel's family. Reheuel became the governor of Gath Odrenoch and protected that city for most of his long life. He watched as it developed and grew into the bastion of human culture and trade for which we now remember it and died at the fine age of one hundred and seventy-five. Tressa followed him a short while after, and they were both outlived by eleven of their twelve children.

"Geuel and Hefthon traveled to the Capital in the winter following their adventure with the smoke fairies. Hefthon served his four years stationed in the Capital where he married and began a family. Afterward, he traveled to

Elicathaliss with his family and there formed a religious order known as the Keepers, soldier-servants of Innocence dedicated to protecting the City of Youth. For nearly a thousand years Hefthon led the Keepers, becoming the oldest living immortal.

"Geuel joined the cavalry and traveled to and from the Capital for years, earning a reputation for valor while fighting fire sprites in the Northern Wastes. He stayed in the cavalry long after the end of his four years and eventually became a colonel at the age of forty. By fifty, he had drawn the attention of the emperor and become a personal favorite. In his sixty-second year, using power granted him by the emperor, he founded a new military order known as the Guards, an elite force led by immortal officers and based in Gath Odrenoch.

"Veil became an apothecary, apprenticing for years in the Capital. Later, several decades after Geuel had formed the Guards, the emperor tasked Veil with the formation of a new medical order known as the Healers.

"All three orders founded by the children of Reheuel lasted nearly as long as the Iris, the Guards and Healers playing vital roles in all of its many wars.

"Less is remembered of Reheuel's later children than of his first three. Most became officers in the Guards. Several followed Veil into the Healers. The youngest, Elivar, inherited his father's distaste for imperialism and traveled to Kheshan where he spent his life studying the technologies of the gnomes.

"As for Ariel, the Fairy Queen aged slowly and lived nearly as long as Hefthon, dying a peaceful death a few decades before the start of the Hunter Wars. Mercifully, she was spared the sight of her city's end. After the city fell, Brylle led what remained of the fairy people on a great migration over the southern jungles, searching for a new home beyond the borders of Rehavan.

"Randiriel never again set foot in Elicathaliss. She traveled to the Capital and stayed there for many years, working as a messenger for the court and earning a name for her wit and cunning. Weaving herself into the politics and intrigues of the court, she earned a title and a place in the Capital's governing body. Geuel remained her close friend during his years as an officer, and they were long remembered for their active roles in the nationalist party.

"After Geuel's death by poison at the age of one hundred and twenty, Randiriel left the court, disillusioned with the Iris and tired of the nobility's petty intrigues. She spent the rest of her life traveling Rehavan in search of some lasting cause, an ideal that she could believe eternal. Her name surfaces in stories for centuries after."

A heavy clatter of wooden poles and metal stakes sounded outside, and the story-man smiled at his listeners. "Well, my friends, I hear them tearing down the tents, and so I know our time is over. I will leave you all to return to your lives and thank you for your ears. Farewell."

The audience slowly drifted from the big tent, staring about in wonder as the other tents began to fall, canopies drifting down and stakes rising from the earth. Groups of elves and gnomes yelled and squabbled along the streets, fighting over the proper ways to pack the materials.

Another circus was over, and the next day all of the story-man's audience would return to their mines and farms, sweating out their weary lives. Their brief respite of wonder had ended.

Beautiful nymphs of the river,
Beautiful sprites of the wood,
Your story now is over.
Return to your forests and floods.

Final stanza of "The Lay of Reheuel"

Note from the Author

Hello, my dear readers, and thank you for lending me your time and attention. I hope what I've given you was enjoyable. It was a small tale, a tale with low stakes and small adventures, without world-ending cataclysm dangling like Damocles' sword above our tortured heroes.

I feel there are too many such stories told, too much made of apocalypses and ultimates. If all a hero ever faces are world-ending scenarios one after another, there can be no ramping up. There can be no increase, no growth. I believe that, even in fantasy, the key to beauty is found in characters, the key to meaning, to pleasure. So, I have built my series upon a foundation of local adventure, of tribulations vital to those enduring them, but small in the scope of the world. From here, the stories will grow. Some will be grand. Some will encompass wars and struggles of gods. Others will be small. But all will hold meaning to those who live them.

If this story brought you any pleasure, any delight, any value, then I beg you, please consider leaving a review on Amazon. I cannot emphasize enough how helpful it is every time a reader takes the extra five minutes to rate or review my work. It makes all the difference in the world for my chances of success.

Wishing you delight and joy in the beautiful world we have all been given, in your lives, those precious gifts bestowed only once upon us all. Wishing you well. Wishing you peace.

With love, Justin Rose.

Made in the USA
Monee, IL
20 March 2023